Dear Reader,

I'm so excited to be a part of Harlequin Flipside! I've always loved romantic comedy because sometimes life is pretty absurd, and all you can do is laugh and go on. I think that's what my character Lucy Lake does. When life hands her lemons, she attempts to juggle them. The results aren't always pretty, but she manages to see the humor in every situation...even when she's falling in love.

I especially enjoyed writing this book because of Millie. I'm a big dog lover, but for some reason I'd never written a story with a dog as one of the main characters. Granted, Millie isn't an ordinary dog, but she does embody that wonderful loving, accepting spirit all dogs have.

So I hope you enjoy *Life According to Lucy*. And look for other Flipside stories from me in the coming months. I love to hear from readers. You can e-mail me at cindi@cindimyers.com, visit me online at www.CindiMyers.com or write me in care of Harlequin Books, 225 Duncan Mill Rd., Don Mills, ON M3B 3K9, Canada.

Happy reading!

Cindi Myers

Lucy hated meeting people before noon!

And now she had to go meet one about flower beds.

She staggered to the kitchen, but she didn't see the old gardener. Instead, she saw a guy with broad shoulders and thick blond hair. She froze. This was definitely a man who would notice her wrinkled shirt and rat's-nest hair, not to mention her leg stubble.

She backed toward her room. She'd just go change clothes, wet her hair and blow it dry, shave her legs, put on makeup—

"Lucy! There you are." Great. Outed by her ever-so-helpful father.

Trapped, she moved her legs automatically as she stared at the gorgeous stranger. He had on more clothes today, but there was no mistaking those broad shoulders and that smile. It was the hot guy who had witnessed her humiliation yesterday. And it looked as if he was about to go two for two!

Life
According
to Lucy

Cindi Myers

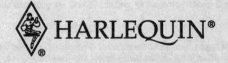

HARLEQUIN®

TORONTO • NEW YORK • LONDON
AMSTERDAM • PARIS • SYDNEY • HAMBURG
STOCKHOLM • ATHENS • TOKYO • MILAN • MADRID
PRAGUE • WARSAW • BUDAPEST • AUCKLAND

ISBN 0-373-44184-3

LIFE ACCORDING TO LUCY

This edition published by arrangement with Harlequin Books S.A.

® and TM are trademarks of the publisher. Trademarks indicated with
® are registered in the United States Patent and Trademark Office, the
Canadian Trade Marks Office and in other countries.

Visit us at www.eHarlequin.com

Printed in U.S.A.

ABOUT THE AUTHOR

Cindi Myers believes in love at first sight, good chocolate, cold champagne, that people who don't like animals can't be trusted and that God obviously has a sense of humor. She also believes in writing fun, sexy romances about people she hopes readers will fall in love with. In addition to writing, Cindi enjoys reading, quilting, gardening, hiking and downhill skiing. She lives in the Rocky Mountains of Colorado with her husband (whom she met on a blind date and agreed to marry six weeks later) and two spoiled dogs.

Books by Cindi Myers

HARLEQUIN TEMPTATION
902—IT'S A GUY THING!
935—SAY YOU WANT ME

HARLEQUIN BLAZE
 82—JUST 4 PLAY
118—RUMOR HAS IT

For Carole,
and other daughters who miss their moms

1

Gardens teach us many lessons, among them humility, hope and the importance of pest control.

WHAT DOES A GIRL have to do to change her luck? Lucy Lake thought as she watched her landlord march past her and deposit her TV by the curb. She'd wanted true love and dated a string of players. She'd wanted a raise and gotten a pink slip. She'd wanted love letters in the mail and instead had gotten an eviction notice. Honestly, how much worse could it get?

"Mr. Kopetsky, it was just a little mix-up at the bank." She followed her landlord back toward the apartment. Could she help it if she hadn't kept very good track of her finances? It had been all right when she'd been gainfully employed, but the money she brought in doing temp work since she'd been laid off hadn't been enough to cover the shopping habit she'd acquired in more flush times.

"Ha!" Kopetsky spat into the oleanders that flanked the walk, narrowly missing the gardener who was planting a flat of marigolds alongside the shrubs. "That check bounced all the way to San Antonio. And it wasn't the first time either." He started up the outside stairs toward Lucy's second floor rooms, pausing to lean over the railing to address the gardener, "Make sure you use that big bark mulch so it don't blow all the way to Del Rio when the wind comes up. I ain't payin' for that stuff to blow away."

"I'll take care of it, Mr. K." The gardener rose, all six feet two inches of him, broad shouldered and bare chested. Even given her distress over her current situation, Lucy couldn't help gaping at him. Her notoriously fickle libido gave signs of stirring, and the only thought that came into her mind was the old soup slogan: *Mmm, mm, good!*

"Can I help you with something, ma'am?"

Her libido made a hasty retreat and her shoulders slumped. As too often happened, the Greek God spoiled everything by opening his mouth. Not that his voice wasn't nice enough—rich and appropriately masculine—but the word "ma'am" was the killer. She was not a ma'am. Her mother was a ma'am. Her grandmother was a ma'am. She, Lucy Lake, was light-years away from ma'am-hood.

"Ma'am?" He did it again, and took a step toward her. "Are you all right?"

"I'm fine," she snapped, and turned away. Any man who would call her "ma'am" was not anyone she could be interested in, no matter how broad his shoulders.

Kopetsky marched past her with a box of dishes. "I'm just doing my job here," he said. "Don't take this personal or anything."

"Oh, of course I won't take it *personal.*" She raised her voice as he walked away from her. "Why would I take having all my belongings dumped by the curb *personal?*"

She was keenly aware of the gardening god standing there watching this little drama. It was bad enough being evicted without having Mr. Bronzed Muscles looking on. She gave him what she hoped was a quelling look, but he annoyed her further by smiling. A gorgeous, white-toothed grin that might have been sexy if not for the fact that it was completely ill-timed.

Kopetsky hunched his shoulders up around his ears and turned to glare at her. "You'd better call somebody to haul this stuff away before trash pickup in the morning."

She frowned. If she didn't get her belongings out of here by nightfall, they'd be picked clean long before the garbage men showed up.

Sighing, she gathered up an armful of clothing and headed toward her car, ignoring the curious looks from her neighbors and passing strangers. Didn't they have anything better to do than gape at her?

Of course they didn't. An eviction ranked right up there with the Mosquito Festival and the Art Car Parade in her neighborhood. All three were venerable Houston entertainments, though mosquitoes and Art Cars had to settle for being feted only once a year.

Other women might have burst into tears or made a big scene, but Lucy was almost getting used to this kind of setback. Two months ago, she'd lost probably the best job she'd had to date when the software company she worked for went belly-up. Since then she'd worked a series of temporary jobs and drowned her sorrows with hefty doses of shopping therapy.

Okay, so maybe those trips to the mall were a bad idea, but a girl's gotta find solace where she can, right? It wasn't as if she had a man she could depend on. Her last steady boyfriend eloped with a cheerleader over a year ago. Stan said she'd always be a good friend, but she wasn't his idea of the perfect girlfriend. She told him dumping someone was not the best way to keep a friendship going, but he just smiled and chucked her under the chin. Talk about insulting! She hadn't been chucked since she was nine.

Since Stan split she'd dated a bull rider, a motorcycle racer, a construction worker, a performance artist and one angst-filled musician, every one of whom seemed to think she was great to be with as long as she didn't want anything from them—say, a wedding ring.

Now, she'd lost her apartment. It hadn't been much of a place, but the rent was cheap and it did have a nice view of the Transco Tower if you stood on the toilet and craned your head in the right direction.

When was the next disaster going to sneak up and bite her in the butt?

"Where do you want this?" Startled, she looked up to find the gardener standing beside her, holding her television as easily as if it was a cube of foam.

"Uh...just put it in the back seat." She opened the door and he slid the TV into the car. "Thanks," she mumbled.

"No problem." He stepped back and surveyed her car, a bright blue economy model that had seen better days. "You're not going to get much in there."

"No kidding." She slammed the door shut. "I'll figure out something."

"I've got a truck—"

She didn't even know this guy. Why was he being so nice? "Look." She turned to him. "Thanks, but no thanks. I didn't ask for your help."

"No, but you need it."

Great. A know-it-all *and* a buttinsky. Instead of a gardening god, the man was a gardening geek. Give her a rough-around-the-edges bad boy who knew how to mind his own business any day.

She turned and marched back toward the front of the apartment building. Garden-boy followed. Honestly, some people couldn't take a hint.

Mr. Kopetsky was depositing a mangy-looking ficus at the curb. "You ought to leave this one for the garbage," he advised. "It looks dead."

"It is not dead!" She reached out to steady the little tree and a rain of yellowed leaves fell to the sidewalk.

"Too dry. And probably not getting enough light." The gardener reached out and felt a brittle leaf. "It's hard to get the conditions right in these little apartments."

She rolled her eyes. "Who asked you, okay?"

He held up his hands. "No one. Just trying to help."

"If I want your help, I'll ask for it."

"Yes ma'am."

"And don't call me ma'am."

"What do you want me to call you?"

"Nothing. Go back to playing in the dirt."

"My, don't you have a way with words?" Still grinning, he retreated to the marigolds.

She stared at his back, at the muscles that gleamed with sweat and swallowed hard. Maybe she'd been a little harsh. He was probably a nice guy. Too nice. No tattoos or piercings, hair clipped short. He looked like the poster child for clean-cut American.

Exactly the sort of man her mother would have loved. Mom was big on clean-cut and polite—men, she said, who had integrity. "You can count on a man with integrity," she'd always said.

Thanks to Mom, Lucy knew what it was like to date an Elvis impersonator, a one-eyed pizza delivery driver and a man who made his living as a sewage plant diver—all of whom were up to their nonpierced earlobes in integrity. She knew her mother's heart was in the right place, but she'd always preferred guys who were a little more exciting than that. Guys who took risks. The kind her mother never approved of. Her motto was: Life Is Too Short to Date Dull Men.

She stared morosely at the ficus. Okay, so maybe it was a tad unwell. Still, she couldn't bear to get rid of it. Her mother, in one of her many attempts to improve Lucy, had given her this tree.

Mom had also given her a bread maker she'd used once, a sewing machine that had never been out of the box and a complete set of the works of Beethoven. She couldn't bear to get rid of any of them either. Now that Mom was gone, she cherished everything associated with her, from half-dead plants to impractical appliances.

Mostly what Mom had given her was advice. "Be patient and one day you'll find the perfect career. One that takes advantage of your unique talents."

"You mean there are jobs out there for women who can read e-mail and talk on the phone at the same time?" she'd asked.

"Your perfect job is out there somewhere," Mom said, ignoring Lucy's lame humor. "And the right man is waiting for you, too. All you have to do is open your eyes and look."

"If I open my eyes any wider my eyeballs will fall out." Could she help it if the dark and dangerous men who got her motor running weren't exactly husband material?

Mom gave her that long-suffering look she'd perfected. "You'll see I'm right one day. I have experience with these things."

What experience? Her mom got married when she was twenty, had Lucy when she was twenty-five and worked part-time in the county tax office until she got too sick to do it anymore. Her life didn't look anything like the one Lucy lived.

She carried another load of clothes and the battered ficus to the car. She liked to think if Mom had beaten the cancer, she'd have listened to her more. But in her more honest moments, she knew that wasn't true. She wasn't the kind of person who took advice, good or otherwise.

When she got back to the curb, the gardener had disappeared. It figured. A man who was truly interested wouldn't have given up so easily. In his place, two women in polyester pedal pushers were pawing through her possessions. One of them held up a lamp she'd inherited from her Aunt Edna. "I'll give you five dollars for this," she said.

Five dollars for a lamp whose base was carved like a pineapple? "Sold!"

"How much for this box of Tupperware?" The second woman held up a carton of kitchen supplies.

She swallowed. "Uh...five dollars?"

Fifteen minutes later, she'd sold the sofa, two kitchen chairs, a toaster that didn't work and a blender that did. She had over a hundred dollars in cash and people were still shoving money at her.

Beep! Beep! She looked up and felt sick to her stomach as a familiar blue pickup truck rolled toward her. Talk about bad timing.... The window glided down and her father leaned out. Dad had thick salt-and-pepper hair that he'd worn in a flattop since he was discharged from the Army in 1969. He dressed in bowling shirts and baggy khakis dating from the Nixon presidency, and shiny cowboy boots. Her friends who met him for the first time thought he was hip and fashionable. She didn't have the heart to tell them he'd been dressing this way for forty years. "Honey, why didn't you tell me you were having a yard sale?" he asked.

She stuffed the cash in the pocket of her jeans and reluctantly walked over to him. "Uh, it's not exactly a sale, Dad."

He stared as two men walked past him with her couch. "You're selling your sofa?"

She pretended to adjust his side mirror. "Dad, what are you doing here?"

"I thought I might take you out for a decent meal."

Since her mom had died a year ago, her dad dropped by a couple of times a week to take Lucy to dinner. He said he wanted to make sure she got a good meal every now and then, but she knew it was really because he was lonely.

A woman marched past carrying her old bedside table. "If you're not having a yard sale, what *are* you doing?"

She stared at the ground. "I've been evicted."

She braced herself for the storm she was sure was coming. The familiar "at your age you should be more responsible" lecture. But he didn't say anything.

After a minute, she couldn't stand it anymore and risked looking at him. He didn't look angry at all, just tired. Old. An invisible hand squeezed her chest. "Is everything okay, Dad?"

He sighed. "I was going through some of your mother's things today."

The hand squeezed tighter. "Oh, Daddy." She touched his arm, not knowing what to say. How did you comfort someone when they'd lost the person they'd lived with for over thirty years?

He gripped the steering wheel with both hands. "There's a bunch of stuff in the potting shed—bulbs and plants and all kinds of books and stuff. I figure I ought to do something with it, but I don't know what."

Lucy's mom had been an avid gardener. She'd won Yard of the Month so many times the Garden Society gave her a brass plaque and told her she couldn't enter again. She'd tried to pass her green thumb along to her daughter, but Lucy was probably the only person in the world who once actually killed a pot of silk flowers.(She forgot and watered them. The stems rusted and they fell over.)

"I thought maybe you'd come over and help me," Dad said.

"Sure. Sure I will." She glanced back over her shoulder

toward her dwindling pile of possessions. She needed to poll her girlfriends to find out who would let her crash for a few days until she could find a new apartment. And she'd probably have to break down and balance her checkbook to see what she could afford. "Uh, how about one day next week?"

Dad opened the truck door and climbed out. "Come on. I'll help you get the rest of your stuff. You can move in with me."

"I don't know, Dad." She followed him over to where two women were arguing over her DVD player. "I wouldn't want to impose." Besides, there was something so pathetic about a single, unemployed twenty-six-year-old having to move back in with her father, wasn't there?

"You got somewhere else to go?" Dad elbowed the two women out of the way and picked up the DVD player.

Her shoulders sagged. "No." She gathered up a box of CDs and followed him to the truck. Unemployed... evicted...back under Dad's thumb. Yep. Trouble came in threes, all right.

GREG POLHEMUS hung the little brass plaque on the wall behind the cash register and stepped back to admire it. *Best of Show, Downtown Art Fair* it proclaimed in fancy script. It looked pretty good up there with the other awards and citations he'd collected lately.

"Your father would be so pleased." Marisel rested her hand on his shoulder and gave him a fond look. The Guatemalan nursery worker mothered everyone at Polhemus Gardens, but especially Greg, despite the fact that he was her boss.

"Oh, he'd probably gripe about me wasting time at an art fair when we have so much work piling up." He smiled, picturing his father in scolding mode. He'd frown and shake a finger at Greg, but his eyes would be dancing with laughter. Greg had never thought he'd miss his father's litany of complaints, but now that the old man was gone, he found himself wishing he'd paid a little more attention to what he'd had to say.

"He would gripe, but he'd still be proud." Marisel impaled a stack of order slips on the spindle by the register. "It's after six o'clock on a Friday night. What are you still doing here?"

"What does it look like I'm doing?" He picked up a sheaf of invoices. "I'm working."

She shook her head. "You need to hire someone to help you with all this paperwork. You can't do everything."

He laughed. "Are you trying to fill my father's shoes in the griping department? You're going to need more practice."

She frowned. "A handsome young man like you should be out enjoying himself. Dancing. Seeing the girls."

When had meeting women stopped being easy? He didn't want to go hang out at bars by himself, and the buddies he used to hang with were either married and raising families or still living like frat boys, sharing apartments and living on beer and fast food. He was stuck somewhere in between, with a house of his own and a business to run, but no family to share it with.

He thought of the woman he'd met today outside the apartment, the one being evicted. Most of the women he knew would have dissolved into tears at the very thought of such public humiliation, but this one had been reading the riot act to crusty old Leon Kopetsky. Then she'd lashed out at *him* like a cobra.

He should have known better than to step into something that wasn't his business, but she'd looked so alone, standing there with all her possessions piling up around her. He'd wanted to do something to help. It didn't even matter that she didn't want his help. There wasn't any real heat behind her anger, only wounded pride. Too bad he didn't have the chance to get to know her better.

He could ask Kopetsky her name, but what good would that do? It wasn't like he had time to spend trying to track down his mystery woman.

"You should go out, meet someone nice," Marisel prodded.

"I see plenty of women," he said. "I was digging a new rose bed for the Lawson sisters just this morning. And Margery Rice calls me at least once a week to come over and see her."

Marisel made a face. "The Lawson sisters are old enough to be your grandmothers and Margery Rice should be ashamed of herself, a married woman flirting like that."

"Oh, I don't take her seriously." He paged through the invoices. Margery Rice was a very well-built forty-year-old who had let it be known he could leave his shoes under her bed any time, but he didn't have any intention of taking her up on her offer. Still, it had been a while since a woman had warmed his sheets. Marisel was right; he needed to make more of an effort to find someone.

"I promise I'll get out and circulate," he said. "After the art show is over and I win the bid for Allen Industries."

"If those people have any sense you'll win the bid. But your father tried for years to get them as customers and he never could." She shook her head. "That shows right there they aren't too smart."

He nodded. Yes, his father had gone after Allen Industries for years. But this year, Greg was determined to get the job. "There's no way they can turn me down. The plan I outlined for them is exactly what they're looking for, and no one will beat the price."

"And then what? You'll spend all your time making sure the job is done perfectly instead of getting out and having any kind of life." She wagged her finger at him in a fair imitation of the old man. "You're too young to be a hermit."

"Yes, ma'am." He bit the inside of his cheek to keep from laughing. At six-two, he towered more than a foot over Marisel, but she looked for all the world as if at any moment she'd lay him over her knee and tan his hide.

"You laugh, but don't you know the woman for you isn't going to fall out of the sky?"

"I was thinking I might find her hiding behind a rose bush one day."

"Why would you think a *loco* thing like that?"

"Pop always said you could find all the best things in life in gardens."

She made a clucking sound with her tongue. "I don't think he meant women."

"You never know. He might have." The way things were going, Greg figured he had as much chance finding a woman in a garden as he did anywhere else. And he spent more time in gardens. He opened a drawer and shoved the invoices inside. "Come on. I'll drop you off on my way home."

She pulled her sweater close around her. "You don't have to go to any trouble for me. I can take the bus."

He slipped his arm around her shoulders. "Come on. If you see any likely looking women on the way, you can point them out to me."

She swatted at him. "You are a bad boy, Greg Polhemus."

"Yes, ma'am. I work at it."

He laughed as she began muttering under her breath in

Spanish and led the way to the car. When he'd caught up on some of his jobs, he *would* make more of an effort to date. That house of his needed a family in it and he was tired of sleeping alone.

2

To dig is to discover.

LUCY COULDN'T BELIEVE she was moving back into her old bedroom at her age. She was supposed to be a strong, independent young woman. So what was she doing letting Dad rush to her rescue? She stared at the antique white bed and dresser her mother had picked out when Lucy turned ten. Her DVD player sat on the dresser next to the ballerina jewelry box Mom had given her for her thirteenth birthday. The bookcase in the corner held her collection of *Sweet Valley High* books and troll dolls.

She half expected her high-school best friend, Janet Hightower, to call and ask her for her notes from history, and had she seen that rad new guy in chemistry class?

She sighed and sank down onto the bed. Somehow, when she'd been planning her future, she'd thought she'd have been past all this by now. In fact, if the diary she'd kept when she was twelve had been accurate, she'd be living in a fifteen-room mansion in River Oaks with two perfect children, a millionaire husband who worshiped the ground she walked on and gave her diamonds "just because" and a silver Porsche in the driveway.

Which just goes to show that at twelve, she hadn't known squat about real life.

She ran her hand along the end of the bed. When she bent

over and pressed her nose up against the quilt, she could smell the faint scent of White Shoulders. Her mother's favorite perfume. What was Mom up to now? Was she a young woman again, swooping around Heaven and flirting with all the men? Was she in some star-dusted greenhouse developing a new strain of tulip? Was she looking down wondering how the heck her daughter had managed to screw up her life—again?

"I'm going to get it together, Mom," she said, in case Mom was listening. "I'm working on it."

Mom laughed. Okay, it was only her imagination, but she knew if Mom was here, she *would* laugh. After gardening, Mom's second favorite hobby was her daughter. "I'm going to find you the perfect man, don't you worry," she'd say.

Lucy groaned, remembering. Her mom's idea of Mr. Perfect and hers hadn't quite meshed. Lucy wanted men who flirted with danger. Bad boys who made her pulse race and her heart pound. Her oh-so-conventional childhood had made her long for darkly handsome rebels.

"Lucy! Where are you?"

"Back here, Dad."

Her father appeared in the doorway, the ailing ficus in his arms. "I think this is the last of it," he said.

"Thanks, Dad." She stood and set the ficus by the window, then stepped back to survey her home-away-from-home. Except for the tree and the DVD player, it looked like she'd never left.

"So where are you working these days?" Her father took her place on the end of the bed.

"Um, I'm still doing temp work until I can find something more permanent." She began unpacking her suitcase.

Dad made a noise that could have been a grunt. "I didn't send you to college so you could do temp work."

She gave herself credit for not rolling her eyes. "I'm an English major, Dad. Houston is full of English majors waiting tables and tending bar. There just aren't that many jobs that call for quoting Emily Dickinson and analyzing Thomas Wolfe."

"You ought to let me talk to the guys down at the hiring hall. They could get you into an apprenticeship program." Dad was an electrician. "There are lots of single guys down at the hall," he said. "You might meet somebody nice."

"I don't want to meet somebody nice." She deposited an armful of T-shirts in the dresser and reached for the next stack.

"You want to meet somebody rotten?"

She smiled and shook her head. "I don't want to meet anybody." Not anyone her father would introduce her to. His idea of Mr. Right was probably even more straitlaced than her mom's.

He leaned forward, worry lines etched on his forehead. "Honey, is there something you're not telling me?"

"What do you mean?" She moved over and unzipped her garment bag.

"You say you don't want to meet men. That doesn't mean you want to meet women, do you?"

She dropped an armload of dresses. "No! Jeez, Dad!"

"I mean, not that I would care or anything. Not that I understand that sort of thing, but—"

"Daddy, I am not a lesbian." She blushed. This was not the sort of conversation she ever pictured herself having with her father. She slid back the closet door and the scent of White Shoulders engulfed her. She blinked at the familiar houndstooth jacket in front of her. "What are Mom's clothes doing in my closet?"

The bed creaked as he stood and came to stand behind her. "She started keeping some of her things in here after you moved out." He cleared his throat. "Guess I haven't gotten around to cleaning them out yet. I can move them into the attic if you want."

He reached for the jacket, but she stopped him. "No, that's okay." She shoved the jacket and the clothes behind it to one side and hung her things on the rod. "There's still room for mine. It'll be okay."

She looked at her cropped, red leather jacket next to her mom's old houndstooth. Mom had never liked that jacket much, but now Lucy thought the two of them looked right at home together.

"Let me call the hall." Daddy interrupted her reverie. "At least you could get a decent job out of it."

She shook her head. "I don't want to be an electrician."

"Why not? It's good, honest work. Kept a roof over your head and food in your mouth for plenty of years."

She turned away and rolled her eyes. Looked like she was in for lecture number seven on Dad's top ten hits. So much for thinking the rent here was free. She'd forgotten about the listening tax.

She made a show of looking at her watch. "Gosh, look at the time." She smiled brightly. "What should we have for dinner?"

"Don't worry about me. I'm going out." He turned toward the door. "I'd better get a move on or I'll be late."

She followed him down the hall. Her first night home and he was going out? "I thought we were going to go through the potting shed tonight."

"You do it, hon. I'm going out." He disappeared into the bathroom at the end of the hall.

Out? Her dad? She shrugged and wandered into the kitchen. The refrigerator held a quart of milk, a wedge of green cheese, half a package of sliced ham that was drying out around the edges, a jar of pickles, a twelve-pack of Bud and three Diet Sprites. The cabinets yielded some crackers, a can of tomato soup, a box of Lucky Charms and a jar of peanut butter. *Lucky Charms?* She hadn't eaten those since junior high.

She was digging into a big bowl of sugar-frosted oats and marshmallows when Dad came out of the bathroom. A cloud of Brut preceded him down the hall. She let out a whistle when he appeared. He'd traded in the khakis and bowling shirt for starched jeans and a striped western shirt with pearl snaps and gold stitching around the yoke. Light bounced off the glossy surface of his boots. "So what do you think?" he asked.

"I haven't seen you this dressed up since Aunt Edna's third wedding." Comprehension slowly stole over her sugar-charged brain. "You're going *out*," she gasped.

He reached for a western-cut sports coat. "That's what I said."

"I mean—you're going out with a *woman*."

He grinned. "Yeah. Don't wait up for me." He kissed her cheek, then left, the scent of Brut trailing after him.

She slumped in her chair, feeling as if she'd slipped into some alternate reality. Her dad? On a date? Mom had been gone only a year—wasn't that a little soon? Only yesterday he'd been a grieving widower. Now he was all decked out like Garth Brooks, telling her not to wait up for him.

She carried her cereal bowl to the sink and dumped the contents down the drain. Who was this woman anyway? Some floozy he met in a bar? He'd been married to her mother for thirty years—what was he doing dating someone else?

Part of her realized she was being totally irrational. Her dad was a grown man. He had a perfect right to date.

The thought did nothing to make her feel better. This was her *dad*. Dads didn't date. Okay, some did, but not *her* dad.

Then an even worse realization hit her. It was Friday night and she was home alone, while her *dad* had a date.

On this pathetic note, she opened a beer and wandered out the back door to the potting shed. Her parents' house used to be a carriage house for the big Victorian next door, which now housed a hair salon, a new age bookstore, a pottery studio and four upstairs apartments. A six-foot high wooden fence separated the two properties, though Mom had had lattice panels installed in two places so the folks next door could look in on her garden.

The showiest flower beds were in the front of the house, devoted to an ever-changing array of colorful annuals. But the backyard was home to Mom's prized roses. She had over thirty bushes in every color imaginable, including a purple rose that was almost black. All the roses had names, which Mom had tried to teach Lucy, but of course, she couldn't remember most of them now.

The potting shed resembled a kid's playhouse, with real glass windows on either side of a bright blue door. Lucy guessed this was appropriate, since it was sort of her Mom's playhouse. She shoved open the door and the scent of potting soil and peat, mingled with undertones of White Shoulders, engulfed her. She swallowed a lump in her throat even as she glanced toward the workbench that ran along the back of the shed. She almost expected to see Mom there, up to her elbows in dirt, grumbling about aphids or spider mites or something.

But of course, she wasn't there. Only a jumble of clay pots, seed packets, fertilizer spikes and flower stakes crowded the workbench. She took a deep breath and stepped into the shed. The least she could do was try to get the place in order.

She set aside her beer and began stacking the clay pots. On a shelf, she found an old shoe box that held seed packets filed in alphabetical order. Ageratum, alyssum, asters, bachelor buttons, basil... She recognized the flowers from the pictures on the front. Probably some of these were meant to be planted in the beds out front, but which ones?

Underneath everything else, she found a spiral-bound notebook with a picture of a Japanese pagoda on the front. *Garden Planner* was embossed in gold beneath the pagoda. She smiled, recognizing a Christmas gift she'd given to Mom several years before.

She pulled an old bar stool up to the bench and opened the planner. *Important Numbers* was the first page. Along with numbers for garden club members, seed companies and a local nursery was the following notation, in Mom's clear handwriting: *When in doubt, call Mr. Polhemus!!*

Mr. Polhemus was a leathery-skinned old man who tilled the beds each spring and delivered mulch for the roses. Mom swore by his gardening knowledge. During those last six months, when the chemo left Mom too weak to plant, he'd even come over one Saturday and set out the fall annuals.

The planner was divided into months. Mom had made notes to herself for each month. Lucy flipped though the pages until the notation for September caught her eye: *Always remember the importance of having a plan.*

Was Mom talking about gardening or life? She frowned. Maybe her problem was she didn't have a plan. After all, would a person with a plan be sitting at home—in her *dad's* home—alone on a Friday night?

She turned the pages in the book until she found a blank sheet of paper, then fished a pen from an old soup can in the corner of the workbench. *Number one,* she wrote, then chewed on the end of the pen, trying to decide what was most important.

Get a decent job, she wrote.

Number two: Find a decent man.

She looked at her list. Okay, so maybe she could stand to include a little more detail. Like what constituted "decent" in either category.

She closed the book and shoved it aside. It was all too much to think about right now. In one day she'd endured the humiliation of being evicted, then been forced to move in with her father, of all people. To add to her misery, her supposedly still-grieving dad was now out on the town with who knows what kind of scheming floozy. Honestly, why was all this happening to *her?* Had she been cast in some new kind of reality show? *Sleeze-o productions presents, How Low Can You Go! starring the lovely Lucy Lake as Hapless Victim number one!*

She wandered out into the garden. The streetlight on the corner cast a soft glow over everything. Traffic over on the Loop was a low hum, in harmony with the fountain that bubbled at the center of the yard.

Her feet crunched on the oyster-shell path Mom and Mr. Polhemus had installed two years ago. The beds themselves were outlined in white rock Mom had collected at a quarry near Austin. The roses were arranged by type: chinas in one section, teas in another, climbers in a third. Normally at this time of year, the bushes would have been covered in blooms, the air awash with the scent of roses.

Unfortunately, Lucy wasn't the only one missing her Mom. The roses looked like they were in mourning, too. Their leaves drooped and the few blooms she found were riddled with holes from marauding bugs.

Mom had planted her favorites in a bed along the back fence. She stared at Mom's pride and joy, a huge pink rose named Queen Elizabeth, a sick feeling in her stomach. It was hardly more than a thorny cane, its few leaves a sickly yellow. Mom would have a fit if she saw this.

She knelt and began yanking weeds from around the Queen, anger adding strength to her efforts. While her dad was out gallivanting around town with who knows who, it would be up to her to look after Mom's garden.

She was struggling to uproot a stubborn clump of grass when a movement near the fence made her scream and jump back. Visions of giant rats or gophers filled her head as she frantically looked for some weapon. People weren't kidding when they said everything is bigger in Texas. Houston's tropical heat and humidity grew nasty pests not seen outside of horror movies.

A snuffling noise from the shadows called forth a whimper from her paralyzed throat muscles. *Oh God, please don't let it be a rat.* Or a possum. Or a mole. Or...

The almost-naked rose canes vibrated as something pushed past them. She jumped back. Where was a good-sized tree when you needed one? Rats didn't climb trees, did they? What about possums? "Go away!" she shouted, and made shooing motions in the direction of the flower bed. "Get out!"

The creature, whatever it was, kept right on coming. She knew any minute now it would burst from the bushes and charge straight at her. She would have run, but her legs refused to listen to her brain. If she ever did get going, she'd probably trip and land face-down on the path. The only thing worse than confronting a rat was confronting one on its own level.

She glanced toward the trellis windows in the fence, hoping to see one of the neighbors out for a stroll. Preferably carrying a weapon—hey, this was Texas, it could happen—but the alley was empty. She took a deep breath. Obviously, she'd have to look out for herself. So what else was new?

The only thing available was the clump of weeds in her hand, so she threw that in the direction of the movement.

In horror she watched as a small shape shuffled out from beneath the rosebushes. It raised its head into the light and looked at her, a pair of beady brown eyes peering out from beneath an overhang of orange-red curls. "Woof" the dog said, and shook mulch from its curly coat.

3

Little problems have easy solutions; for big problems, it's probably too late.

LUCY'S ADRENALINE SURGE abandoned her, leaving her weak-kneed and feeling a little foolish. A dog? She'd been terrified of a dog?

Not just a dog, she amended as the canine in question shuffled closer. A poodle. A toy poodle. Evidence of a long-ago trim still lingered in the pom-pom on the end of its tail and its overgrown topknot.

A flood of sympathy drove out the last vestige of fear. "Oh, baby, how did you get in the backyard?" She glanced toward the alley gate, but it appeared to be latched. She squatted down and held out a hand to the pup. "It's okay. You don't have to be afraid of me."

The next thing she knew, the pooch had its front paws on her knees and was licking her in the face. Who needed makeup remover with a dog like this? "Okay, okay!" She held the dog at arm's length, fending off sloppy kisses. (Reminded her of a few guys she'd dated.) She checked for a tag and collar—no sign of either. While she was at it, she took a peek between its legs. "So you're a girl. That's good." Considering her track record, the last thing she wanted was another stray male in her life, even of the four-legged variety.

She set the pup on the ground and stood. "I'll bet you're hungry."

"Woof! Woof!" The pup raced toward the back door and stood with her nose pressed against it.

She laughed. "I take that as a yes." The pup raced ahead of her into the kitchen. She opened a cabinet and started shuffling through the contents. "We don't have any dog food. I don't suppose you'd like a can of soup, would you? Or Lucky Charms? I think I remember seeing a can of tuna fish...."

When she turned around, tuna in hand, she saw that her furry visitor had somehow managed to open the refrigerator and was busy demolishing the rest of the sliced ham. The dog made loud smacking noises and wagged her tail at Lucy.

"If you hang around long, I guess we'll have to buy a lock for the refrigerator." She shut the door and dropped the shredded ham wrapper into the garbage, then filled a bowl with water and set it down for the dog. The pup attacked that with enthusiasm too, managing to splash water in a foot-wide radius around the bowl. When it finally raised its head, water dripped from its ears and chin.

Lucy opened a Diet Sprite and leaned against the counter, studying her visitor. "I guess I should take you to a shelter."

The dog sat up straighter and gave her a reproachful look. The kind of look that made her want to plead guilty to some crime she hadn't committed. "I thought only mothers could look at you that way," she muttered.

"Okay, so I guess the shelter idea is out. But I'll have to call around and make sure nobody is looking for you. You're kind of a cute dog for somebody to abandon."

The dog rewarded this comment with a tail wag. Lucy sat at the kitchen table and the dog climbed into her lap and began the face-washing routine again. She tried to fend her off and checked the clock. How did it get to be after ten? And where was her dad?

He probably hadn't been out this late since the Milligan's New Year's Eve party two years ago. What if he got tired and fell asleep at the wheel on the way home? What if all this socializing was too much for him and he had a heart attack? What if a drunk driver crashed into him...?

What if he decided to spend the night with his mysterious date?

She pushed the dog away, clutching at her own chest. Maybe the pain she felt wasn't a heart attack, but it was definitely a heart ache. "Don't go there. Do not even think about it." After all, parents didn't really have sex lives, did they?

"Woof!"

The pup cocked its head to one side and looked up at her. "What do you know about it?" she asked.

You know you have sunk to a new low when you spend a Friday night talking to a stray dog. What was worse, she actually imagined the dog looked sympathetic.

She tried watching TV, but all that did was put the dog to sleep. While the pup snored on one end of the sofa, Lucy went out into the potting shed and retrieved her mom's garden planner. Maybe something in there would tell her what to do for the ailing roses.

The book was full of notes about gardening, all written in her mother's careful hand. But she didn't see anything that would help her save the roses. She found information on when to prune (missed that one already) and when to spray (missed that one, too.) Nothing about what to do with sick roses.

Of course not. The roses were never sick when Mom was alive.

I'll bet that gardener I met today would know what to do. She shook off the thought. She didn't even know the guy's name, and it wasn't as if she had any intention of going near Kopetsky again to find out.

She continued flipping through the book. *August 15: plant fall tomatoes and asters. Order pyracantha and euonymus for new bed along driveway. Buy vitamins for Lucy.*

She smiled. Mom was always telling her to take her vitamins. To bundle up when it was cold. To think positive. She used to view her advice as meddling. What she wouldn't give to hear it all again.

With a sigh, she flipped the book shut, but it fell open again to the phone list at the front. The underlined words leapt out at her: *When in doubt, Call Mr. Polhemus.*

Of course. Mr. Polhemus would know what to do about the roses. She reached for the phone and dialed the number. No one would be in this time of night, but she could leave a message. "Polhemus Gardens, Leave a message and I'll call you back." Mr. Polhemus's voice was a familiar growl on the answering machine.

"Hi. This is Lucy Lake—Barb Lake's daughter. Her roses aren't doing very well. I wonder if you could come over and take a look at them? It's an emergency. Thanks."

She felt a little better when she'd hung up the phone. At least she'd done *something.* The dog woke up and crawled into her lap. Her fur was soft as silk and her tummy was warm against Lucy's thighs. All in all, she found the animal's presence strangely comforting.

DAD FOUND THEM there on the sofa, asleep, when he came in. Lucy woke, heart pounding, when she heard the door click shut. "Who's there?" She demanded, clutching the dog to her chest. As if a fifteen-pound poodle would be much protection.

The light came on and Dad stood in the doorway. "I told you not to wait up," he said.

Meanwhile, the dog proved her watchdog capabilities by lunging toward Dad and launching herself at his chest. "Woof!" But the effect was spoiled by her wildly wagging tail and lolling tongue.

"Who is this?" Dad ducked away from the dog's kisses.

"She was in the backyard. I guess she's lost or abandoned."

"Friendly little thing, isn't she?" He scooped her up and handed her to Lucy. "And you found her in the backyard?"

"Yes. She was back behind the rosebushes."

He chuckled. "Just what we need, another redhead who's crazy about roses."

Lucy glanced at the dog. Her hair *was* the same color as her mother's. Her gaze shifted to the clock and she came instantly awake. "Dad, it's almost three o'clock!"

He grinned. "Yeah, can you believe it?" He stretched and yawned. "I'm beat. I'm going to bed."

She stared after him as he shuffled down the hall. She wanted to call after him, to demand he tell her what he'd been doing, and with whom. She frowned at the dog. "I don't like this. And I don't like that I don't like it. What kind of a lousy daughter am I anyway?"

The dog whined and laid her head against Lucy's arm. This must be why people like dogs so much, she thought. No one will adore you the way a dog will. They don't care if you don't look good or make a lot of money or if you have evil thoughts. Keep the dog biscuits coming and they'll love you for life. If only men were so simple.

ENTIRELY TOO FEW hours later, Dad was pounding on the bedroom door. "Lucy, wake up! Greg Polhemus is here to see you."

She surfaced from beneath the covers, grunting. "What time is it?" She mumbled and groped for the clock.

"It's seven-thirty."

Why did he sound so cheerful? She hated people who were that cheerful before noon. "What does he want?" She stifled a yawn and slid back down under the blankets.

"He said you called him."

"Hmmm. Yeah. I guess I did." Who cared about old Mr. Polhemus when this bed was so nice and comfy....

"Aeeeee!" She leapt out of bed, swearing and lunging around for the cruel person who would stick an ice cube in her side when she was trying to sleep.

How about a cruel dog? And it wasn't an ice cube, but a cold, wet nose. The pup sat on Lucy's pillow and wagged its tail, the doggy equivalent of a grin on its face. "What are you so happy about?" Lucy snapped.

"Woof!"

She figured that remark had something to do with breakfast. Not bothering to look in the mirror, she ran a brush through her hair and pulled on the shorts and T-shirt she'd worn last night. Every time she'd seen Mr. Polhemus, he was in the same stained coveralls and dirty ball cap, so he wasn't likely to notice what she had on.

When she staggered into the kitchen, her dad was sitting at the table with a guy who had broad shoulders and thick blond hair. The stranger was laughing at something her dad had said and didn't see her coming in. She froze in the doorway. Why hadn't Dad mentioned Mr. Polhemus had brought a *man* with him? A man who might possibly notice her wrinkled shirt and rat's nest hair, not to mention her leg stubble.

She backed toward her room. She'd just duck in, change clothes, wet her hair and blow it dry again, shave her legs, put on makeup—

"Lucy! What are you doing back there? Come on out and meet Greg."

Her legs moved automatically as she stared, goggle-eyed, at the man with her dad. He had on more clothes today, but there was no mistaking those broad shoulders and that smile. "Greg? You're Greg Polhemus?"

He smiled and stood. "If it isn't Miss Nothing."

He actually *stood up*. Her mother would love that. Of course Lucy had known that already, hadn't she? But where was the real Mr. Polhemus? "What happened to the old man in the coveralls?" she blurted.

His smile faded. "That was my dad. He died last year."

Okay, could they just rewind and start over? She gulped. "I'm sorry." That's the way she liked to start every day— shoe leather for breakfast.

She dropped into a chair and the dog immediately vaulted into her lap. "Cute dog," Greg said.

"Uh, yeah." She rubbed the dog behind the ears. Anything to keep from looking at him. "Yeah. She showed up last night. I think she's lost."

He leaned over and patted the dog's flank. He smelled like Irish Spring. The dog's tail beat against Lucy's side. "Maybe somebody dumped her," he said.

Some man, she thought. She scratched the pup's chin. "I guess if no one claims her, I'll keep her." *After all, we women have to stick together.*

She stifled a yawn and risked a peek at Greg. Okay, so maybe he wasn't a total geek. He hadn't given her too hard a time about yesterday. At least not yet. And he did have nice hair and bronzed muscles and all... He looked up and caught her staring. She fought back a blush. "Do you always start work so early?"

He shrugged. "You said it was an emergency."

"Well, yeah. It's my mom's roses. They're dying."

"What's wrong with them?"

"I don't know. That's why I called you." She was easily annoyed in the morning. Especially when she was operating on only four hours sleep. "Or rather, I called your dad." She frowned at him. "Do you know anything about roses?"

He stood, towering over her. "I know *everything* about roses."

She bit back a groan. Lord save her from arrogant men!

GREG FOLLOWED Lucy out into the backyard. She wasn't exactly what he'd expected from Barb Lake's daughter. Barb had been the stereotypical suburban housewife, in sweater sets and khakis. Her daughter looked like she'd stepped out of the pages of some hip fashion mag. Or rather, she looked like a model who'd slept in her clothes. She'd obviously just rolled out of bed. The thought sent a kaleidoscope of erotic images whirling through his brain.

He focused on her cute little bottom as she picked her way along the garden path. She was acting all bent out of shape because he had shown up instead of his dad, but he figured it was mostly a face-saving move, considering the last time he'd seen her she'd been literally tossed out on the curb.

He dragged his gaze away from her to study the yard. Sun glared off the oyster-shell paths and heat radiated off the fence boards. The thermometer on the wall showed eighty-two degrees.

Then his gaze landed on the roses and his stomach twisted. The bushes looked as if they'd been attacked by locusts. The canes drooped and drifts of yellow leaves decorated the mulch. Barb must be turning over in her grave. The old man was probably spinning right along with her. He moved closer and broke off a remaining leaf and examined it, then dug down into the mulch with his fingers.

Lucy fidgeted beside him, like a patient waiting to hear the worst.

He moved to another bush, and then another, shaking his head and making clucking noises under his tongue. This was bad. Really bad.

"Well? What's wrong?" Lucy blurted.

He straightened and turned to her. "More like what isn't? You've got black spot, aphids, powdery mildew, root rot and rust." He ticked the maladies off on his fingers.

She blinked at the pathetic plants, her mouth trembling. He braced himself for tears. Did he have a clean handkerchief anywhere?

"Can't you do something?" she asked.

He looked at the roses again and sighed. "Maybe. It'll take a lot of work." Just what he needed. More work.

"That's okay."

Sure. A babe like her probably *had* a social life. "Um, what I meant to say is it will take a lot of *my* work."

"Oh." She traced a dollar sign in the oyster shell with the toe of her sandal. "Are you expensive?"

"I can be." He grinned, unable to resist adding, "But then, I'm very good."

She jerked her head up to stare at him and he gave her a lazy, half smile. Maybe trying to resuscitate Barb Lake's roses wouldn't be such a hardship. Especially if he could talk her daughter into working with him.

A noise in the bushes distracted them both. That little dog of hers was digging furiously in one of the beds. "Looks like the pup's ready to get started," he said.

"Hey! Get out of there!" She lunged and the dog darted away.

"What are you going to call her?" Greg asked.

She brushed aside the shower of leaves that had drifted

onto her arms and shoulders when she'd gone after the dog. "I don't know. I haven't thought about it."

"You found her in the garden. It ought to be something to do with gardening. How about Rose?"

She wrinkled her nose. "Rose doesn't sound like a dog's name."

He looked around, seeking inspiration on the shelves outside the potting shed. Ortho—no. Daconil— He didn't think so. *Mille fleur* fertilizer... He grinned. "How about Millie?"

She looked down at the dog. "I think I like it. What do you think, Millie?"

The dog's ears drooped and she let out a low growl.

"I don't think she likes it," Greg said.

"Well, I do." She scooped the dog into her arms. "From now on, I'm calling her Millie."

He glanced around the garden again. "I'll have a crew out on Monday."

"Can't you start today?"

He shook his head. "I have other jobs. This is going to take some time." Although he didn't know how much time the roses had left.

"What can I do to help?" she asked.

"You can pull all the mulch away." He gestured to the beds. "We'll need to dig out everything, put in new soil, prune, spray, fertilize...."

Her shoulders drooped and she cuddled Millie closer. "Uh, okay. I guess we'll wait until Monday then."

He grinned. "I'll see you then."

"Oh. Well, I'll probably be at work."

He thought he did a pretty good job of hiding his disappointment. "Where do you work?"

"Here and there." She waved her hand in the air. "I'm

between jobs right now, so I'm doing temp work until I find something in my field."

"That must be interesting."

"It's not. Most of it bores me out of my mind, but it pays the bills. Some of them, anyway." She glanced back toward the house. "It'll be good for me to stay here a while, to, uh, help out my dad, you know."

"Yeah." He'd moved back home the last few months of his father's life. It had been a strangely disorienting experience, but one he didn't regret.

They stood there for a moment, alternately looking at each other and the half-dead garden. Even disheveled with no makeup, she was beautiful. She had short, spiky dark hair and big green eyes with long dark lashes and delicate features. Not a conventional beauty maybe, but she definitely stirred something in him.

"Well...uh, I'd better let you be going," she said finally. She took a step back toward the house. "See you around."

"Yeah. See you."

She let him out the back gate. He made himself walk to his truck without looking back, but he was sure he felt her gaze on him. When he reached the truck, he risked a glance in her direction. She was still there at the gate, the dog in her arms, a pensive look on her face, as if she was trying to figure him out.

"Then that makes two of us," he said softly, and climbed into the truck. *If you come up with any answers, be sure to let me know.*

Lucy watched Greg drive off and waited for the overheated feeling inside her to vanish. She'd obviously been alone too long if an arrogant geek like Greg could make her all hot and bothered. With any luck she'd have a job on the other side of town Monday and she *wouldn't* see him at all.

She went back inside and found Dad gathering up his keys and wallet. "Dad, where are you going?"

"I'm meeting a friend for brunch."

She sniffed the air. The distinct smell of Brut wafted over her. "The same friend you were with last night?"

He grinned. "No, a different one." He kissed her cheek. "See you later."

"Great, my dad has a better social life than I do." Millie didn't offer any sympathy this time. She was still staring after Lucy's dad, a funny look on her face.

Lucy decided to call shelters. Not that she really wanted anyone to claim Millie, but she figured she had to make an effort, in case the pup was some child's dog. She didn't want to be responsible for some kid crying herself to sleep every night for the next week.

"Hello, Noah's Ark? I have a poodle that wandered into my yard last night.... It's a toy poodle, about fifteen pounds... Her hair is orange. Well, not really orange, sort of pinkish orange.... Oh, all right then, apricot.... No one's reported a missing apricot toy poodle? Thank you." She left her number, just in case, and moved on to the next listing.

Six shelters and not one had a report of a missing apricot poodle. She set down the phone and smiled at Millie. "Well, girl, looks like we're stuck with each other."

"Woof!"

So now should she spend a Saturday morning home alone doing laundry, or should she try to scare up a little fun? As if the washing machine wouldn't still be there tomorrow. She decided to do something productive—her nails. She was adding the second coat of Marvelous Mauve when the phone rang.

"Hello?"

"What are you doing answering the phone at your parents' house? Is something wrong?"

"Hello, Gloria." She rolled her eyes. Gloria Alvarez was her oldest and dearest friend, and the one person who wouldn't let her get away with anything. "Why are you calling my parents' house?"

"I called your number and got a recording that said it had been disconnected. Then I tried your cell and no one answered. I stopped by your place and there's some old guy with no teeth sitting in your living room."

"It's not my living room anymore."

"What? You got a roommate?"

"No, I've been evicted."

"Evicted? Kopetsky did that to you? How dare he!"

She smiled. That was Gloria for you. Ready to leap to a friend's defense without a second thought. If Lucy let her, Gloria would be organizing a picket line to patrol the sidewalk in front of her old apartment and writing irate letters to the *Houston Chronicle.* "I think it had something to do with the fact that my rent checks kept bouncing."

"Oh." A long silence while she pictured Gloria taking a slug on her extra-large chai with soy milk. "Listen, if you're a little short right now, I could loan you—"

"That's okay. I appreciate it, but I'm doing okay. Really. I just need to keep track of things better." And maybe cut down on shopping...but no, she'd catch up on everything as soon as she found a real job again.

"So where are you living now? I'd offer you a place, but with Dennis and the girls there's no room." Dennis was Gloria's boyfriend, a struggling comedian who supplemented his income by teaching at a comedy defensive driving school. The idea was, if people had to sit through eight hours of traffic laws and driving techniques, at least make it entertaining. Dennis might never have a future on stage, but his presentation of the top ten ways to avoid a traffic ticket had people rolling in the aisles. The girls were a pair of greyhounds Gloria adopted from a rescue organization. Their names were Sand and Sable, tall elegant dogs that looked almost comical walking alongside short, round Gloria.

"That's okay. I have a place to live."

"Where? Don't tell me you moved in with that musician. I told you he's no good for you."

"That musician" was an angst-ridden aspiring country star Lucy had dated for a few weeks. He only knew three chords on the guitar and he sang with a twang that would peel paint, but he looked spectacular in a pair of starched jeans and a cowboy hat, so Lucy had no doubt he'd go far. Gloria had hated him on sight.

Gloria hated all the men Lucy dated. She claimed to be able to read in the tarot cards that these men weren't good enough for her friend. Maybe she was right, since no man had been good for her yet. "No, I moved back home. Just until I get back on my feet again."

She was sure Gloria would have lots to say on this subject, none of it good, but her friend surprised her. "That's a good idea," she said. "It's healthy to get back to your roots sometimes. Home is a good place to heal."

"Gloria, I'm not sick."

"Maybe not physically, but spiritually— Listen, I have a new book to lend you. It's called *Karmic Healing* and the woman who wrote it..."

Lucy sort of tuned out the rest of what Gloria had to say. So sue her. Gloria had a new theory about life every week. She was into crystals, fortune telling, feng shui, aura reading and ancient Native American rituals. Only last week, she'd told Lucy ten different ways to realign her chakras.

As for Lucy, if a theory didn't involve shopping or chocolate, she wasn't interested. "I have to go, Gloria. I, uh, I think someone's at the door."

"Wait, wait. I have to tell you the reason I called. My friend Jean has a booth at the downtown art fair and I told her I'd stop by. Wanna come?"

"Sure. I'm into art." Anything was better than washing her father's shorts. "And afterwards maybe we could swing by the mall...."

Gloria laughed. "Okay. Pick me up in half an hour."

4

Making simple matters complex or complex matters simple are both bad gardening techniques.

LUCY LEFT MILLIE with a breakfast of canned tuna and a fresh bowl of water. She made a mental note to buy dog food and something more substantial than dry cereal for herself while she was out today. After she'd backed the car out of the garage, she glanced back and the dog was watching her out the window like an abandoned child. *I don't need this kind of guilt*, she thought.

Gloria and Dennis shared a duplex off Gessner. It was one of those areas of the city that used to be run-down but was now trendy. Slick new apartments sat side by side with sagging bungalows. Gloria claimed this gave the neighborhood character. Personally, Lucy thought it meant paying high taxes and still having to dodge the crack-house traffic on weekends.

But Gloria and Dennis had fixed up their place and it looked real nice, if you didn't mind purple burglar bars on the downstairs windows and a red front door. When Lucy pressed the door bell, she set off frantic barking, accompanied by the scrabble of toenails on the hardwood floors. Gloria opened the door and Sand and Sable launched themselves at Lucy with all the enthusiasm of body surfers in a mosh pit. She fended off doggy kisses and lashes from doggy tails. "Yes, I'm thrilled to see y'all too," she said as Gloria dragged them by the collars back into the house.

Dennis appeared in the hallway, a container of instant ramen noodles in his hand. "Hey, Lucy. What are you chicks up to?" Like many men in their late twenties and early thirties, Dennis had his hair cut very short in an attempt to disguise the fact that he was going bald. Unfortunately, he also had rather large ears, one of which sported a gold loop. When he wore a white T-shirt, as he did now, he bore a startling resemblance to Mr. Clean.

"I told you, we're going over to see Jean's display at the art festival." Gloria made a face at Lucy. "He never listens."

"I listen." He stabbed at the noodles. "I just don't agree that what Jean does is art." He pointed the forkful of quivering noodles at her. "She makes collages out of garbage."

"It's *found* art," Gloria corrected.

"Garbage."

Lucy hated it when her friends fought. She never knew what to say and besides, the argument was usually over something really uninteresting. It wasn't as if she could actually get involved in the conversation. "How did it go at the *Laugh Stop* last night?" she asked Dennis.

"Lame crowd." He spoke around a mouthful of ramen. "They wouldn't know funny if it bit 'em in the ass." He dropped the fork into the ramen container and set it on the hall table. "Gotta go. Got a class this afternoon." He aimed a kiss in the direction of Gloria's cheek. "Catch you chicks later."

When he was gone, Lucy helped Gloria put the girls in the backyard. "How was your first night back at home?" Gloria asked.

"Okay, I guess." She waited while Gloria locked the various deadbolts on her front door. "My dad went out on a date."

"A date?" She grinned. "I think that's sweet."

Lucy led the way to her car. "Gloria! It's only been a year."

"But your mom was sick for a year before that. I mean, he must have been lonely. Besides, your dad's kinda cute. If I didn't have Dennis—"

Lucy clapped her hands over her ears. "You did not say that. I do not want to hear my best friend lusting after my dad."

She opened the car and they both slid in. "Speaking of lust, is there a new man in your life?" Gloria asked as she fastened her seat belt.

"No. Why would you think that?"

"Your aura has a nice warm red tone today. Signifying sexual arousal."

Lucy rolled her eyes. The things Gloria believed. "I do not have a new man in my life." She pulled the car into traffic and headed downtown.

"Auras don't lie. You haven't met anyone new? Even casually?"

"No. Well, not unless you count the gardener I hired to try to salvage my mom's rose garden."

"Oh? Is this a male gardener?"

She thought of Greg Polhemus's well-defined muscles and broad shoulders. "Uh, yeah."

"Then he counts." Gloria angled toward Lucy and assumed her therapist's tone of voice. "Tell me about him."

She shrugged. "What's to tell? His dad always took care of my mom's garden. I got his number out of her garden planner. But then the old man's son showed up instead."

"What happened to the old man?"

"He died. About the same time as my mom."

"See, there's something you have in common."

"Gloria, I am not lusting after this guy. He's a gardener and that's it."

"Is he good-looking?"

She squirmed and tightened her grip on the steering wheel. "I suppose. If you like the clean-cut, straight-arrow type."

"And, of course, you don't."

"Come on, Glor. Have I ever gone in for guys like that? You know I dig men who are more exciting. Dark and dangerous."

"Maybe that's why you're still single." She held up her hands in a defensive gesture. "I'm only saying auras don't lie. You ought to think about this guy more."

"All I'm thinking about is whether or not he's going to save my mom's roses. You should see them. They're pathetic. Mom would cry."

Gloria leaned across the seat and patted her hand. "It'll work out. Things always do."

Easy for someone to say who already had a job *and* a man she loved.

They snagged a parking place a couple blocks from the festival and followed the crowds toward the plaza that had been taken over by artists' booths. Lucy could have found her way with her eyes closed by following the smell of corn dogs, funnel cakes and sunscreen that was the particular perfume of any outdoor festival.

In addition to food and artwork of every description, the booths featured an array of handmade items, from intricate beaded jewelry to crocheted doilies no extra roll of toilet paper should be without.

Halfway down the first aisle, she spotted a booth advertising homemade doggie treats. She grabbed Gloria's arm. "Wait, I want to get some of these."

"You don't have a dog." She followed her into the booth.

Lucy grabbed up a plastic bag and began filling it with bone-shaped cookies. "I do now. She showed up in the garden last night. An apricot poodle. I named her Millie."

"How sweet. That's a very good sign, you know, that she chose you for her new home. Animals have good instincts about people."

"Glor, it's a stray dog. She was in our yard. Where else was she supposed to go?"

Gloria spread her arms wide. "Maybe this is the universe's way of telling you you're about to begin a series of new relationships."

I'd settle for one good relationship with a member of the opposite sex, she thought, but she didn't dare tell Gloria that. She might start in on Greg Polhemus again.

They found Jean's booth in the second aisle. Jean worked at the crisis center with Gloria when she wasn't assembling art from trash. Lucy studied a piece displayed at the front of the booth. It featured a penny, a dime, a gum wrapper, a cough drop covered with fuzz and a ball of lint formed into something resembling a tornado, in which the aforementioned items whirled. *Wash Day Blues* was neatly inscribed in ink across the bottom.

"It's a collection of all the items I found in my pockets while doing laundry," Jean explained, coming up behind her. "Clever, huh?"

"Uh, yes." But would anyone actually pay for it?

While Gloria and Jean discussed the significance of garbage as a cultural indicator, Lucy wandered across the aisle to a booth displaying beaded jewelry. Now this was art she could relate to. She picked out a black-and-purple choker and carried it over to the mirror to try it on. She'd about decided she had to have it when a movement in the mirror caught her eye. A woman in a tight leather miniskirt,

fringed tank top and hot-pink cowboy boots was waving a
peacock feather fan around like she was Gypsy Rose Lee
while a gray-haired man in starched jeans and ostrich boots
looked on.

Her stomach took a dive toward her ankles as her numb
brain finally registered that the guy was her dad and the
woman was someone she'd never seen before in her life.

She dropped the choker and whirled around, gasping for
air. Gloria ran over to her. "Lucy, what's wrong? Your face
is so pale. And your aura..." She stepped back and fur-
rowed her brow. "Honey, your aura looks really bad."

Who gives a flying fig what my aura looks like? She felt like
shouting, but some invisible hand had a hold of her throat
and all she could do was point in the direction her dad and
his "date" had headed.

When she could talk again, she told Gloria she'd seen her
dad with a strange woman. "Come on, we have to follow
them." She took off after them, past a booth full of pottery,
a caricature artist and a display of batik clothing. She finally
spotted them at the funnel cake booth. Little Miss Leather
was breaking off bits of fried dough and feeding them to
her dad, who obediently opened his mouth like a toddler
playing the airplane game.

She grabbed on to the corner post of the sausage-on-a-
stick hut, feeling sick to her stomach.

"C'mon, Loo. What's the big deal? He's just having a little fun."

"Gloria, that woman is *my* age."

She tilted her head to one side, considering this. "Oh, I
think she's a little older than that. Thirty, at least."

"That's still twenty-five years younger than my dad.
And look at the way she's dressed."

"That leather looks awfully warm for this time of year.

But the boots, very retro. I wouldn't mind a pair for myself."

Lucy glared at her. "Whose side are you on anyway?"

"I have to choose a side? I didn't know we were having a fight."

She clenched her hands into fists. "We aren't, but we will be if you keep insisting on defending that bimbo."

Gloria shook her head and made a tsking sound. "Now, be rational."

"I don't want to be rational!" Honestly, what was rational about this situation? This was her *father* they were talking about, not some stranger. A man who had spent almost every Saturday for the past ten years at the hardware store or watching sports on television. Why was he suddenly chasing around after a woman half his age?

"You don't even know her," Gloria said. "She might be very nice."

She took a deep breath. This was one of the things she didn't understand about life: just when she thought she was all grown-up, a sensible, mature woman, something like this would happen to make her feel like a six-year-old. The thought of throwing a temper tantrum was eerily satisfying at the moment.

About that time the woman in question started sucking the sugary remnants of the funnel cake off her fingers with an enthusiasm that caused her dad's eyes to glaze over, and Lucy's brief stab at maturity to flee. "I don't care if she teaches kindergarten to underprivileged children and spends Sundays volunteering at the nursing home," she growled. "I don't want her dating my father."

The couple started off walking again and Gloria and Lucy followed at a distance. They were holding hands now, her father standing so erect, shoulders squared and chest out, that Lucy wondered how he could breathe.

It wouldn't be so bad if he dated someone his own age, she thought. Someone sweet and motherly. But what did a bombshell like this gal see in a fifty-five-year-old man? Okay, so he was in pretty good shape for his age, but honestly... What if she was trying to scam him? Dad would be easy to take advantage of. After all, he'd been out of the dating scene a long time. He didn't know what it was like out there. Things were bound to have changed a lot and he'd be an easy mark for some unscrupulous bimbo.

Dad and the woman stopped at a booth selling ceramic masks. While she admired one of the fanciful creations, Dad turned to face Lucy and Gloria, gazing idly around. Lucy ducked into the large tent to keep from being seen.

The tent featured all kinds of bushes and trees growing in pots and cut into fanciful shapes. "Topiaries," Gloria said, admiring a baby elephant sculpted of ivy. "These are very nice."

Lucy peeked out from behind a penguin made of privet. "Are they still over by the masks? I can't see."

Gloria glanced behind her. "They're still there."

Lucy moved up, still keeping behind the displays in case Dad looked this way again. "What are they doing?"

"I think she's trying to convince your father to buy one for her."

"I knew it! She thinks he's her next sugar daddy."

"Good afternoon, ladies. May I help you?" A smiling, older Latina woman approached. "That is a beautiful poodle, isn't it?"

Lucy stepped back and realized she'd been lurking behind a larger-than-life sized rendition of a poodle. "Uh, yes. Yes, it is." She thought of Millie. Why hadn't she stayed home with her today instead of ending up in this mess?

"Are you looking for something in particular?" the sales-woman asked.

She shook her head. "Uh, no. We're just looking."

"Uh-oh," Gloria hurried to join her behind the poodle. "They're headed this way."

The saleswoman looked confused. "Is something wrong?"

"No. Everything's fine." She retreated further into the tent. "We'll have a look over here."

"Over there!" Gloria nudged her and pointed to a sign marked Maze.

She followed her into the maze, which had been formed out of pots of clipped hedges. The only problem was, the hedges were only chest high. They had to crouch down to stay hidden. Which meant her butt was sticking up. Not the most attractive position.

"I think this must be for kids," Gloria said.

She peeked over the top of the maze and saw her dad and the woman enter the tent. Her dad pointed to the poodle and said something that made the woman laugh. She ducked down again, narrowly avoiding being seen.

"Why don't you go out there and introduce yourself?" Gloria said.

She was right, of course. This was a public place. There was no reason she shouldn't walk right up to her father and say hello. Except how would she explain what she was doing in the kiddie maze?

That, and the fact that she was a coward.

"They're coming this way," Gloria hissed.

She tried to see through the bushes, but they were too thick. Then she spotted a gap a little farther down the line. If she spread a couple of branches apart with her hands, she could just fit her head through...there. Now she could see them and she was pretty sure they couldn't see her.

The woman was clinging to Dad's arm as if she might fall over without support and Dad still looked slightly dazed. He was carrying a plastic bag that she guessed held the mask and no telling what other swag she'd talked him into buying for her. *Come over here a little closer*, she thought, glaring at her. *I'll drag you into these bushes and show you what happens to women who take advantage of my father.*

About that time, they turned in her direction and she shrank back. Of course, she had no real intention of getting into a catfight in the middle of the children's maze. She liked to think she was tough, but her real nature had the fortitude of warm custard.

Something on the far side of the tent caught the bimbo's eye and she dragged Dad off in that direction. Lucy heaved a big sigh. While the woman and Dad were occupied elsewhere, maybe she could sneak away.

"Come on, let's get out of here," Gloria said. Lucy felt her crawl past.

She had every intention of joining her friend, but when she tried to turn around, her head wouldn't move. She was wedged firmly in the tightly woven branches. "Uh, Gloria?" she said in a loud whisper.

But apparently Gloria was already too far away to hear her. Lucy wrapped her fingers around the limbs on either side of her neck and tried to pry them apart, but all that got her was scratches on her arms. *Great*, she thought. *I'll be stuck here forever.*

"Daddy, what's that lady doing over there?"

"I don't know dear. Perhaps she lost a contact lens. Let's not bother her."

Yeah right. Everybody looks for contact lenses in the walls of a maze. She guessed it made as much sense as spying on your own father. She pulled back harder, tears stinging her eyes as twigs raked her skin and tangled in her hair.

She could feel sweat running down her spine and making the backs of her knees sticky. Her underwire was cutting a groove into her left breast. And about that time, like a four-year-old on a road trip in the middle of nowhere, her bladder announced that she really did have to pee. Honestly, could things get any worse?

"I've seen a lot of strange things at these art shows, but this has to be one of the most, uh, *interesting*." She froze as the deep masculine voice sounded behind her. The bushes rustled, and then a familiar face was level with hers. "Lucy Lake, what are you doing here?"

She would ever after be able to testify that it was not possible to die of embarrassment. If it were possible, she'd have keeled over right there. Standing there before her in all his muscular, tanned glory was Greg Polhemus. As she glared at him, he threw back his head and laughed.

5

Relax and be still around the bees.

WHEN GREG HEARD the commotion over by the maze, he figured a child had panicked in there, or been separated from mom or dad. The next thing he knew, he'd have some angry parent railing at him, and the ghost of his dad whispering in his ear that this was what he got for being innovative.

He ducked between the waist-high rows of bushes and started toward the first turn in the maze, only to be brought up short by a woman's backside and legs jutting out in the aisle before him.

Not the sort of thing he expected to find lurking among the ligustrum. Of course, he'd always considered himself a leg man. And these were a particularly fine pair of legs, and the backside that went with them was as shapely as any he'd seen. As his eyes traced the feminine curves, his libido reminded him just how long it had been since he'd been in close contact with such a sexy shape. Definitely too long.

"My friend is stuck." A short, round woman hurried up to him. "Do something."

Still smiling to himself, he backed away to get a better look at the rest of this fetching female. His smile turned to laughter as familiar features glared up at him out of the shrubbery. "Lucy Lake, what are you doing in there?"

Despite her ridiculous position, she managed to look affronted. "Never mind that. Get me out of here!"

Still laughing, he turned to head out of the maze. "Where are you going?" The friend called after him. "You can't just leave her here."

"Be right back." He headed for the supply shed where he'd stashed his clippers.

Marisel looked up from the cash register. "What are you doing?"

"I need to do a little trimming in the maze." He flashed a grin and hurried back to Lucy and her friend. And he'd been worried about his work interfering with meeting women. This one kept showing up every time he turned around. "Hold still, I'll have to cut you out."

He carefully maneuvered the clippers to reach the branch that was holding her hostage. She jerked back as the metal tips brushed against her ear. "Be careful with those things!"

"Hold still and you'll be fine."

He bore down on the clippers, slicing through the branch just as Lucy let out a howl that would curdle cream. She pulled out of the maze and staggered to her feet, one hand clapped to the side of her head, her eyes sending him "drop dead" messages.

His heart lurched, and he dropped the clippers and reached for her. "What happened? Did I cut you?"

"Stay away from me." She backed away, her escape blocked by the hedge. When she lowered her hand, her fingers clutched a lock of hair. "Look what you did."

He reached out and took the single dark brown curl. It was soft as silk against his skin. He studied the gap in her hairdo. "Maybe you can comb it over so it doesn't show."

"Only a man would think a comb-over would fool anyone."

"It's okay, Luce." Her friend joined them. "At least you're out now."

She brushed leaves and twigs from her clothes, then looked past him, her eyes searching for something. Or someone. A man, maybe. Greg's mood darkened. So where was this guy when she'd needed help? "What were you doing in there?" he asked.

To his surprise, she blushed. He didn't know many women who did that anymore. "Maybe I was looking for a contact."

He took a step toward her, and looked into her eyes. Deep-set, almond shaped eyes, the color of magnolia leaves. The kind of eyes a man could get lost in. "You don't wear contacts."

She looked away, at the ground between their feet. "It doesn't matter. Look, I'd better—"

"She was spying on her father and his girlfriend."

She glared at her friend. "Why did you tell him that?"

The friend smiled and shrugged. "Because it's true."

"You don't like your father's girlfriend?" He inserted himself back into the conversation, intrigued.

"I don't even *know* my father's girlfriend. Neither does he. He just met her."

The anguish in her voice touched him. He wished he were better with words—one of those people who always knew exactly what to say. The best he could muster was a show of sympathy. "Sounds rough. I remember when my dad started dating again after my mom died."

Her eyes widened as she stared at him. "Your dad dated?"

He suppressed a laugh, knowing she was trying to picture his father, in his gardening coveralls and dirty ball cap, ever dating. "It was a long time ago, but yeah, he dated. It wouldn't have been so bad if the women he chose were anything like my mom, but it seemed like he went out of his way to find women who were the exact opposite of mom."

She nodded. "This woman is almost my age. What could my dad possibly see in her?" She swallowed. "Mom would die all over again if she knew."

"Come on. Let me help you out of there." He offered his hand and after a slight hesitation, she took it. He helped her step over the low wall of shrubbery, his hand lingering on her arm.

She shrugged away, gently, and hugged her arms over her chest. "What happened with your dad?"

"I guess after a while, he decided it wasn't worth the trouble. He settled down and stopped going out." The realization made him sad now, though at the time all he'd felt was relief that his dad was acting "normal" again. "I think...maybe he was just lonely."

She combed her fingers through her hair, vainly trying to cover the gap, and shot him an annoyed look. "Why should my dad be lonely? He's got tons of friends. And he's got me."

"It's not the same, though, is it?" He gave her a long look, wondering what went on in that head of hers. She came across as a ditz sometimes, but he had an idea she had more going on than that. "Aren't you lonely sometimes, too?" he asked. "Even with friends and family around?" He thought of his own empty house and his empty bed, of this ache inside himself he tried to fill up with work. Did Lucy know what that felt like?

She stopped fussing with her hair and looked at him. Really looked at him. For half a minute, their eyes locked and he felt a warm wave of anticipation. Something was happening here....

Then she looked away, and shrugged. Shrugging off the feeling between them, and maybe him, too. What was it with her? It wasn't like he had bad breath or something—was it?

He open his mouth to say as much, but she spoke first. "Why can't my dad find someone closer to his own age? Someone who doesn't have 'gold digger' written all over her?"

"Maybe you should fix him up." *Or maybe you should quit worrying about your dad and go out with me.* He frowned at the thought. As if Miss Fireball here would go out with him. She'd done nothing but flare up at him since they'd met. Which, of course, was part of the attraction. What man wouldn't want a woman who generated such heat, though the fire he was feeling probably wasn't exactly what she'd intended to kindle. Still, there'd been a definite moment between them just now....

Her green eyes lasered in on him again. "What are you doing here? I thought you said you had to work this morning."

"I do. This is my booth." He gestured toward the maze behind them. "This is the most popular attraction at the festival."

He watched for her reaction as she looked around at the topiaries and living sculptures. His dad had never appreciated this kind of "fancy work," preferring to devote himself to roses and ornamental plants.

"It's amazing." The friend spoke up first.

Lucy nodded. "It's pretty interesting." She glanced at him. "I'm surprised."

He stiffened, remembering his dad's disdain for his "hobby." "Surprised that a guy who makes his living digging in the dirt could do something like this?"

She shrugged. "I figured you were the more practical type."

"Just goes to show you don't know me very well."

Their eyes met again, definite heat in the look this time. He wondered if she felt it. How could she not? The air between them practically sizzled. But her expression remained as cool as ever. She was the first to look away. "I'd better go."

"Yeah." He had customers to see to. He didn't have time to stand around all day talking to her. Especially when she obviously wasn't interested. "See you Monday."

She nodded and walked away, the floral and spice scent of her perfume washing over him as she passed. He turned to watch her as she made her way out of the booth, his eyes lingering on the curve of her hips, remembering his surprise and delight when he'd first seen her in the maze.

He stroked the soft curl of hair in his hand. "Who was that?" Marisel came to stand beside him.

"Trouble," he said. "Beautiful trouble." Something he usually avoided. But then again, maybe it was time he invited a little more trouble into his life.

LUCY HELD her head up as she and Gloria left the Polhemus Gardens booth, determined not to let Greg see how much he'd shaken her up.

"What was that all about back there?" Gloria glanced over her shoulder. "Who *is* that guy?"

Lucy elbowed her friend in the ribs. "Don't look. You'll encourage him."

"Why wouldn't you want to encourage him?" Gloria raised her eyebrows like a silent movie star overemoting. "He's a hottie."

She winced and hurried between the rows of booths, putting distance between herself and her pratfall in the privet. "He's the gardener I hired to save my mother's roses."

"That's the gardener? No wonder your aura's looking so good."

So they were back with the auras. Next thing she knew, Gloria would be reading her tea leaves. "He's supposed to be an expert on roses. That's all I care about. Honestly, Glor, do you really think I could be attracted to a man who spends his spare time carving poodles out of shrubbery?"

Up the eyebrows went again. "It's called topiary, and it shows he has a creative side. And it's not any worse than that artist you dated. I never could understand anything he did."

She hated to admit Gloria was right. Greg Polhemus's topiaries were kind of cute. The kind of thing her mom would have gone gaga for. She frowned. "So he's good-looking and creative. He's still not my type."

"Like you know so much. You're not exactly batting a thousand in the relationship game."

Who exactly made that rule that brutal honesty in a friendship was a good thing? "Thanks for reminding me." She scanned the crowd around them for some sign of her father and his cowgirl. She half hoped she wouldn't see them. She didn't feel up to dealing with her father's late-blooming love affair and her own wacky hormones.

Gloria tugged at her arm. "Come on. I'm your best friend. What's the real reason you're so down on that gorgeous gardener?"

She sighed and turned to face her friend. "Besides the fact that he's boring and conventional?"

Gloria shook her head. "I'm not buying a word of it."

She glanced around, half-hoping for some distraction in the crowd. No such luck. She looked at Gloria again. "Okay, look. Even *if* I was attracted to Greg Polhemus— and it's a big if—every time I meet up with the guy I manage to look like a doofus. He probably thinks I'm a total flake."

Gloria's smile could have melted ice cream. "He didn't look like he was sorry to see you."

"Yeah, well, he was staring at my ass." She knew she had it going on in the caboose department—no sense denying it.

Gloria laughed. "That only proves he's a man. You need to lighten up. He's going to be working at your house, why not give him a chance? See what happens. You never know…"

"If I have any kind of luck at all, I'll be working Monday and won't have to see him at all."

"Chicken."

"I prefer to think of it as avoiding the opportunity to make a fool of myself again." She searched the crowd again.

"Your dad and his date are long gone right now," Gloria said, doing her mind reading thing again. She grabbed Lucy's arm and dragged her toward the parking lot. "Come on, let's go to the mall. A little shopping and you'll feel better."

"Okay." Gloria was right. Shopping always made her feel better. As soon as she stepped into the air-conditioned splendor of the Galleria, heard the hum of the crowd and caught sight of the colorful displays in the store windows, her spirits rose.

She might not have a handle on the rest of her life, but give her a credit card and a shopping bag and she'd have an armful of bargains in no time. What did she care what some dumb gardener thought of her when she was surrounded by a dressing room full of killer outfits?

HALF AN HOUR after their arrival at the mall, Lucy stood in the dressing room of Neiman's and studied her reflection in the three-way mirror. The red-and-white polka-dot mini was a great look for her, but was it too tight around the hips? She tugged at the fabric and frowned. It needed something—maybe jewelry...

Her gaze drifted upward and came to rest on the jagged gash in her hair. Irritation churned her stomach. What had Greg been thinking, coming at her with a pair of clippers like that?

And what had she been thinking, crawling into the bushes in the first place? Her shoulders sagged and she began stripping off the dress. No sense wallowing in that embarrassment all over again. Time to destroy the evidence.

She exited the dressing room and found Gloria trying on hats. She looked up at Lucy's approach, a purple felt cloche with a cockade of peacock feathers perched on her head. "What do you think of this one?"

"All you need is a fringed shawl and a crystal ball and you'll be ready for the gypsy carnival." She grabbed her friend's elbow. "Come on, let's get out of here."

Gloria replaced the hat on the shelf and glanced at Lucy's empty hands. "You didn't buy anything?"

"I don't have time for that now." She tugged Gloria toward the exit.

"Where are we off to in such a hurry?"

"The hair salon. I have to fix the mess Greg made of my hair."

Ten minutes of power walking took them to the opposite end of the mall and *Stylissimo*. "Can you work me in?" Lucy asked, panting only slightly from their rush through the mall. "I have a hair emergency?"

The very tall, very thin woman behind the counter raised one carefully penciled brow as she eyed Lucy's ruined hairdo. "What happened to you?"

"It's a long story." *An embarrassing one.* "Can you fix it?"

The woman smiled. "Darling, Bernardo can fix anything."

Right. Even my mixed up life?

While a plump, balding man she assumed was Bernardo fussed over the damage, she attempted to put a positive spin on her experience with Greg thus far. Maybe she'd use it as research to write a book for women who were trying to get out of a pesky relationship: *Fifty Ways to Lose a Lover.* 1. Lose your job. Unemployment is *soooo* attractive. 2. Bounce rent checks and get evicted from your apartment. Make sure Mr. Wrong is there to witness your dramatic exit. 3. Show him your true self by looking like a hag in his presence. 4. Make a fool of yourself in a public place.

If she worked at it, she was sure she could come up with fifty ideas, though she prayed she wouldn't have to personally try them all.

Maybe this was just a phase she was going through, like the six months in junior high when she'd grown so quickly she kept tripping over her own feet or the bad bout of acne that had plagued her in eleventh grade. Any day now she'd wake up and find everything back on track again. She'd have a fab job and a cool apartment and a hot new romance. She'd be so together people would think she'd always been that way.

"You know I'm going to have to cut your hair a lot shorter to fix this mess, don't you?"

Bernardo's question pulled her from daydreams of a glorious future. She smiled up at him. "Go for it. I'm ready for a big change."

6

There are no gardening mistakes, only experiments.

THE ENTRY FOR Barb Lake's gardening journal for the second Monday in June read *Don't be afraid to experiment with new techniques and varieties. Wonderful discoveries are often made by accident.* A note in her mother's handwriting added, *Dinner plate dahlias!!* and *Send sunscreen samples to Lucy. Maybe she'll take the hint.*

Lucy had smiled at the note. Would Mom be happy to know the makeup she used these days contained sunscreen? "It's not that I never did *anything* my mom suggested," she explained to Millie as she dressed for work. "I just prefer to come to my own conclusions in my own time."

The dog tilted her head and appeared to be listening. She wagged her tail, though whether in agreement or general doggie happiness, Lucy couldn't tell.

She was combing gel through her new hairdo when Millie began having a conniption. The dog was barking and running back and forth between the bathroom and the back door, seriously distracting Lucy from contemplating the short, short style Bernard at *Stylissimo* had concocted to hide the damage done by Greg's clippers.

"Calm down, will you?" she shouted, buying a few seconds silence as the dog stared at her. She turned her head to admire the new do from the side. Not bad. Bernard had earned the sixty bucks she really couldn't afford.

In the brief lull as the dog quieted, she heard a car door slam and men's voices. She checked her watch. Seven-fifteen. Who was here at this hour?

Millie resumed barking, even louder this time. "All right, all right, I hear you." She covered her ears and raised the shade on the bathroom window to glance out back. Her stomach did the wave as she recognized a Polhemus Gardens truck. Two Mexican men climbed out, followed by Greg Polhemus, his perfectly cut blond hair glinting in the morning sunlight. Here it was practically daybreak and he looked as if he'd been up for hours.

A faint melody drifted to her and she realized he was whistling. "I don't think I can take this," she mumbled, lowering the shade again. "There ought to be a law against being so cheerful in the morning."

She'd planned to be out the door long before Greg arrived. It was too early in the morning to match wits with him, not to mention the man obviously brought out the worst in her. She gathered up her purse and tote bag and let Millie out the back door. The dog would run right to Greg and distract him. With luck, Lucy could sneak out before he spotted her.

But of course, luck was never with her where Greg Polhemus was concerned. She was tiptoeing to her car when he hailed her. "Good morning." His gaze took in her khaki miniskirt, white baby doll T-shirt and straw platform sandals. "Off to work?"

She shifted her purse to her other shoulder. "The temp agency said I should dress casual."

He leaned over the fence, arms resting on the top rail, his smile positively dazzling. "So what are you doing today?"

"Some kind of merchandising job." She shrugged, pretending she didn't notice the perfect teeth or tan forearms. "Handing out samples or coupons or something."

"I guess it beats sitting behind a desk all day. I never could handle that."

"I don't mind, really." A desk would look pretty attractive about now. Something she could hide behind.

His gaze fixed on her head and she put a hand to her hair, wondering if it was sticking up or something. "I like the new style," he said. "It suits you."

She ignored the warm glow his praise sent through her. Honestly. As if his opinion mattered. "I had to get it cut after the job you did with the clippers."

"You can deduct the cost from my bill." He straightened. "Guess I'd better get to work. Have a good day."

"Yeah. You too." He wasn't so bad, really, for a man who had seen her at her worst. Maybe if they'd gotten off to a better start... She shook her head. Nah. The few down-to-earth types she'd tried dating had either been intimidated by her opinions or annoyed by her attitude. And he'd probably expect her to be able to cook or something like that. Better chalk him up as forbidden territory and move on. The last thing she needed in her life right now was another wrecked romance. From now on, she was looking a long time before she leaped. She was going to find a job and a place to live before she even thought about another relationship. Then she was going to screen all applicants thoroughly. Maybe she'd have them take a compatibility test, like those computer dating services:

Dear bachelor,

In order to determine your suitability as a partner for Lucy Lake, please answer the following questions:

1. Your idea of a dream date involves a) candlelight and wine b) whipped cream and chocolate c) pizza and beer.

2. *You think a woman's place is a) in the bedroom b) in the boardroom c) any place she wants.*

3. *The perfect vacation would be a) a camping trip b) a cruise c) all expenses paid.*

4. *Tattoos are a) an artistic expression b) a matter of individual tastes c) icky.*

5. *Hard work is a) its own reward b) a necessary evil c) over-rated.*

The thought had its merits. Still, the first man who tore the quiz up in her face might be the very man she wanted most. She sighed. Looking for love was like looking for the perfect outfit. Sometimes you didn't know what you wanted until you saw it on the rack.

WHEN LUCY REPORTED to the address the temp agency had given her, a short, nervous man greeted her. "Oh good. You wore something comfortable." He reached into a closet and pulled out a voluminous garment bag and thrust it toward her. "Here's your costume. You're the special guest today at Little Tykes Day Care. Wear the costume and hand out free boxes of our new cereal." He jerked his head toward three cartons stacked by the door.

She poked the garment bag. Whatever was in it had a lot of weird angles. "What's the costume?"

The man crossed his arms and backed away, bumping into his desk. "Didn't they tell you? You're Puffy the Penguin." He made a shooing motion toward the door. "Now go on, you don't want to be late."

Of course he didn't offer to help her with the cartons or the costume. By the time she had everything loaded into the car, sweat was puddling at the base of her spine and her bangs were sticking to her forehead. She consoled herself with the knowledge that Little Tykes Day Care was bound to be air-conditioned. And hanging out with toddlers all day might be a kick. After all, she'd once thought of becoming a teacher. So what if she had to wear a goofy costume? No one would know it was her. She might even have a little fun with her new "secret identity."

When she arrived at Little Tykes, she found an obliging janitor to help her shlep the cereal boxes into the cafeteria, then she returned to the car to don her costume.

The penguin suit must have weighed twenty pounds. Putting it on, she felt like one of those fake sumo wrestlers popular at Spring Break beach parties. Not only was the bird heavy, it was hot. Inside of five minutes, she'd sweated through her clothes. She hoped the AC was going full blast inside Little Tykes.

She studied the head before putting it on. Puffy the Penguin had enormous doe eyes, like those paintings of sad children you could buy on street corners in border towns. His bright orange plastic beak was twisted into a silly grin. In other words, he was completely ridiculous, which probably accounted for his popularity with the under-five set.

"Okay, here goes nothing," she muttered, and shoved the fake head over her own.

The inside of the bird smelled like old gym socks. How many other people's sweat had soaked into this costume? Ugh. She didn't want to go there.

Peering warily from the narrow peephole below the bird's beak, she waddled toward the entrance to Little Tykes. If she could make it there without passing out from the heat, she'd be home free.

She was scarcely in the door when a very tall woman in a gray suit and half glasses rushed toward her. "Where have you been? Everyone's waiting." Without pausing to hear Lucy's answer, the woman grabbed Puffy's flipper—or whatever the stubby appendage was called—and started dragging Lucy down the hall. She had a blurry impression of primary colored walls and pint-size chairs before she and her handler burst through a set of orange double doors into a room filled with children.

At least from Lucy's perspective, the room appeared to be packed with kids. The two inch by four inch opening in the penguin head gave her distorted views of children's heads, arms, legs and the cafeteria tables at which they sat, like snapshots from a camera no one had bothered to focus.

"All right." The woman, who still had hold of the costume as if she expected Lucy to bolt at any minute, leaned down to hiss in her ear. "I'll say a few words, then when I introduce you, say your piece. But make it quick."

"Yes, *Herr Capitan!*" Lucy answered, but the costume muffled the words, so in the end all she could do was nod stupidly. In any case, all she wanted to do was throw the sample boxes of cereal at the rug rats and vamoose. The sooner she was out of this stinky, sweaty pile of fake fur, the better.

"Now children, we have a very special guest this morning. Does everyone know who this is?"

"Puffy Penguin!" a hundred high-pitched voices shrieked.

"Yes, that's right." The woman's voice dripped with artificial sweetness, setting Lucy's teeth on edge.

"Puffy is here this morning to remind us all of the importance of eating a good breakfast," the woman continued.

Lucy thought of her own morning routine of a Diet Coke and a strawberry Pop Tart. Her mother had always been after her to eat something more nutritious.

She had a sudden vision of Greg Polhemus leaning over the back fence, glowing with energy and good health. He probably started every day with a nice bowl of granola. Her mother would so approve.

The dragon lady was still droning on about nutrition.

Lucy leaned back against a cafeteria table, trying to find a way to sit, but the stubby penguin tail got in the way.

"Now Puffy has a special treat for all of you." The woman reached back and yanked Lucy upright. "Everyone, come say hello to Puffy."

High-pitched shrieks echoed off the walls of the cafeteria and seemed to ricochet around the inside of the penguin head. Lucy blinked and staggered back as hoards of pint-size terrors rushed at her, mouths open, eyes wide, screaming "PUFFY!"

Wham! A child slammed against her knees. Another had a death grip on Lucy's—the penguin's—thighs. She tried to move away, but more and more children piled on, clinging to her wings and tail, climbing on her back.

"I love you, Puffy!" one boy yelled in her ear from his perch on the table beside her, effectively deafening her.

Vaguely, she could hear her handler and other adults trying to coax the children away, but their gentle pleading was ignored. The little monsters continued to grope and prod her, drooling on the fake fur, clutching at the costume until Lucy feared they'd rip her limb from limb.

The head of the costume was off-center now, so that she could only see out of one eye. She somehow found the table and groped for the sample boxes of cereal, thinking she would distract the mob with the promise of sugar-coated puffs. But she couldn't grip the boxes with her flippers.

Children pushed and shoved, grabbing up boxes of cereal, ripping them open, throwing them. She grunted as a child butted his head into her stomach. She staggered back, fending off her overzealous admirers as best she could.

The heat was stifling. She felt faint and on the verge of panic. Weakly waving her flippers/wings and bobbing her head, she backed toward the door, dragging clinging children with her.

She pushed out the door, children and teachers following her. She half-stumbled, half-ran toward the exit, pursued by a wave of screaming tots and pleading teachers. Free at last, she burst onto the front steps and ripped off the penguin head, gasping for air.

She could hear screaming and crying, muted now as her head swam and her vision blurred. She blinked, amazed to see a man walking toward her. She knew she was hallucinating now, because she could have sworn Greg Polhemus was standing in front of her. It figured her brain would remind her of him at a moment like this. Lately, Mr. Perfect was always rushing to her rescue.

She sank to her knees and fell over, like a turtle on its back, unable to rise. She lay there, staring up at the sky and expecting at any moment to be trampled to death by hoards of four-year-olds in size two Keds.

"Lucy? Is that you?" Greg's hand on the side of her neck was cool and soothing. She smiled. For a hallucination, this wasn't bad. Now if he'd only pick her up and carry her away from all of this. To someplace cool and pleasant...

She was still smiling when he emptied the contents of a bottle of water over her face.

LUCY SAT UP, sputtering, and Greg knew she was furious. He stepped back, just in case she decided to lash out at him. "What the h—?"

"Careful," he warned. "Lots of little ears around."

She looked at the crowd of teachers and children gathered behind them on the steps, her scowl deepening. A woman in a gray suit stepped forward. "What did you think you were doing, running out like that? I hadn't dismissed you yet. You frightened the children."

"Those children attacked me. I had to get away from them."

Ms. Gray Suit looked down her very long nose at them. "Nonsense. The children were merely enthusiastic. They'll probably have nightmares now about Puffy the Penguin ripping off his head."

"Nightmares! I'm the one who's going to have nightmares." She tried to rise, but the costume made it impossible. Greg helped her to her feet, but kept a grip on her, just in case she decided to launch herself at the long-nosed witch.

The woman sniffed. "I'll be reporting this to your employer."

"You do that," Lucy snapped. "And I'll report you for letting these children run wild."

With a final sniff, the woman turned to herd the children back inside. "Come along everyone. Time to return to your classrooms."

Still fuming, Lucy looked around, apparently in search of a target. Unfortunately, Greg was it. "What are you looking at?" she demanded.

He choked back a laugh and looked away, afraid he would lose it altogether if he met her gaze. Unfortunately, his eyes now focused on her oversize, orange plastic feet. "That's...uh, some costume," he stammered.

She shoved the outfit down over her shoulders and stepped out of it. "It's hot as Hades and smells like a locker room."

He gave up trying to fight back a grin and shook his head. "You're amazing, do you know that?"

She stared at him as if he'd lost his mind. "What are you talking about?"

"I never know what to expect from you."

"Yeah, well, who asked you to expect anything?" She looked more puzzled than angry now. "What are you doing here anyway? Are you following me?" Her eyes narrowed. "Why aren't you at my house, working?"

"I left Sebastian and Arturo pulling out all the old mulch and came here to present a bid for new landscaping on the grounds." He glanced toward the closed door. "I'm thinking now may not be the right time."

"That woman is crazy. The whole place is crazy. I wasn't kidding when I said those children attacked me. I thought they were going to rip me apart in there."

"They were probably excited to see you. I mean Puffy."

She planted her hands on her hips and gave him a look that indicated she'd gladly rip him limb from limb. "Look, could you not be so reasonable? Would it be so hard for you to take my side in this?"

He attempted to look sober, which was hard to do, considering he was arguing with a woman who until moments ago had been dressed as a five and a half foot penguin. "You're right. It was wrong for those four-year-olds to come after you like that. You might have been hugged to death."

She swatted at him, but he dodged the blow and scooped up the costume. "Come on, I'll make it up to you. I'll buy you lunch."

She hesitated, then agreed. "But no cereal. I don't ever want to look at Penguin Puffs again."

He chuckled to himself. "I know I won't." He'd never be able to look at breakfast cereal again without thinking of a certain curvy brunette.

LUCY COULDN'T BELIEVE she was having lunch with Greg. But hey, having completely humiliated herself as Puffy the Penguin, it wasn't as if she had to worry about him making a move on her or anything. And it would give them the opportunity to talk about her mother's garden.

She traced one finger through the condensation on her iced tea glass. "So, do you think you can save my mother's roses?"

"No guarantees. They're in pretty bad shape."

She bit her lower lip. "But you said you were good, right?"

He laughed. "Yeah, but even I can't work miracles." He sat back, his expression thoughtful. "This is really important to you, isn't it?"

She looked past him, feigning indifference. "Well, yeah. I mean, my mom really loved those roses. She'd hate to see them like this."

"She was a real sweet lady. Whenever I'd come over to help my dad, she'd always fuss over us, bring us lemonade and cookies and stuff."

"That was my mom, always mothering everyone." Her expression sobered. "So, uh, I really was sorry to hear about your dad."

"Yeah. Somehow I thought he'd stay around forever."

They were both silent a moment, contemplating their losses. The waitress arrived with their meals. Greg shook a napkin into his lap. "What about your dad?" he asked. "How's he doing?"

She shrugged. "Okay, I guess. I mean, he seems all right. It's hard to tell, you know."

"Still dating the young chick?"

"He goes out almost every night, but I don't think it's always with the same woman." She sighed. "It's not like I don't want him to be happy. I think it'd be great if he could find someone to spend time with. But all this rushing around all of a sudden—it just seems so desperate."

"Sometimes you have to let people make their own mistakes. He'll settle down after a while."

"But I don't want to see him hurt."

"Now you sound like your mother, fretting over everyone."

She stiffened. That showed how much he knew. She studied him over the top of her tea glass. His red T-shirt was faded to the color of brick, the fabric stretched tight over muscular shoulders and biceps. He looked like an ad for a gym. "Do you have any tattoos?" she asked.

He froze, fork halfway to his lips. "What?"

"Do you have any tattoos?"

"No. Do you?"

"As a matter of fact, I do. What about piercings? Do you have any of those?"

He shook his head. "No. Why?"

"Parking tickets? Do you have any of those?"

He laughed. "Everybody has parking tickets."

"Thank God. I was beginning to think I was having lunch with an Eagle Scout."

"Tenderfoot."

"What?"

"I only made it as far as Tenderfoot rank in scouting."

The corners of her mouth insisted on tipping up in the beginnings of a smile. "My mother would have loved you."

"So you don't?"

Why was he smiling like he knew something she didn't? "Let's just say my mother and I didn't have the same taste in clothes or men." She slathered butter on a tortilla. "My mom was the Texas Martha Stewart and I'd rather stand out in a crowd than feed one."

"Oh, you stand out all right. It's hard not to notice a girl in a penguin suit."

She laughed. "Yeah, well, that's not my usual fashion statement. You haven't exactly seen me at my best."

"What I've seen hasn't been bad."

The look he gave her set her senses humming and little

warning bells sounded in her brain. *Danger. Danger. This would not work, remember?* She pushed away her plate. "Thanks for the lunch. I guess I'll see you around."

"Have dinner with me."

He didn't beat around the bush, did he? Okay, so neither would she. She shook her head. "I don't think so. I mean, thanks, but I don't think it would ever work. We don't have anything in common."

"Other than we're attracted to each other."

His gaze met hers and held. She might have stopped breathing for a minute. Since when did a boring guy make her feel this way? She wet her dry lips. "Well, yeah, but that's just physical. You need more than that for compatibility. I mean, you're a nice guy and all, just not my type."

"Uh-huh. And what is your type?"

She squirmed. How to say this and not come off sounding like a freak? "I go for guys who are sort of...unconventional. Action types. Into adventure and stuff like that." *Not like you.*

For some reason, he was smiling even more now. And here she'd been worried he'd be insulted. He reached across the table and took her hand. "I don't believe you're the big bad girl you pretend to be."

She tried to pull her hand away, but he held on, though she figured he'd let go if she really fought. But she wanted to hear what he'd say next, so she stayed put. "Why would I care what you think? You don't even know me."

"I know a bluff when I see one. You talk a good game, but inside you're a cream puff. You're as wild as my Aunt Margaret."

She stiffened. What did he know? "I am not a...a cream puff!" Did he think she was so sweet and bland? She had not one, but *two* tattoos. In college, she'd streaked through the freshman dorm on a dare. She knew how to make twelve different types of martinis.

"Of course, I have to admit, I don't know many woman who end up in the kind of situations I keep finding you in."

What was he grinning about? Was he making fun of her? "I'm sure you think I'm very amusing."

"Oh, I'd have to say your getting stuck in my maze was pretty funny."

As if she'd set out to make a fool of herself around him on purpose. She jerked her hand away. "It's your fault. These things only happen when you're around."

He chuckled. "That must be it. I put a curse on you."

You are a curse! But she wasn't going to argue with him anymore. She threw her napkin on the table. "Don't you have work to do?"

He shoved back his chair. "As a matter of fact, I need to head over to Allen Industries and talk to them about a bid I put in on a project."

Sheesh, he sounded so responsible. So purposeful. She didn't even know what she'd be doing tomorrow. Didn't that prove right there how incompatible they were? "At least my job isn't boring," she said.

"No." He chuckled again and tossed a twenty on the table. "One thing you are not is boring."

"Unlike you." There! She'd let him know exactly what she thought of him.

But instead of being offended, he only grinned more. "But not when you're around."

She turned away, unable to look at him anymore. If she didn't know better, she'd swear he was *flirting* with her. Courtship by insult. Now that was a new one for her. "Take me back to my car."

"All right." He took her arm and gently steered her toward the door. "But I'll be keeping an eye on you. I can't wait to see what happens next."

His touch made her feel as if she'd suddenly swallowed Mexican jumping beans. Her brain told her to move away, but her body refused to obey. She cleared her throat. "Um, have you ever *considered* getting a tattoo?"

Laughter danced in his eyes, beneath a definite heat. "When I'm around you, I consider all kinds of things I never thought about before."

There went the jumping beans again. What a time for the laws of attraction to kick in! Honestly, you'd think she *enjoyed* his solicitous attitude. As if she *needed* someone to look after her!

7

Sometimes the real value of a garden is determined by what it doesn't contain.

"WHAT YOU NEED is to get out and meet some new people," Gloria said when Lucy told her about the Puffy the Penguin fiasco. "Expand your horizons. Make new opportunities."

"You sound like my mother. This morning her gardening journal advised me to 'clear paths and trim back useless brush.'

"How Zen. Your mother was very perceptive."

"She was talking about gardening, not life." She shook her head. "What I need is to find a job. One that doesn't involve wearing a costume." That, and for her father to start acting normal again, and her mother's roses to bloom. Then maybe she could think about finding a new man—one who saw her as fascinating and smart and competent.

Gloria frowned and shook her head. "With all the negative vibes you're sending out right now, you're not going to attract anything positive. You need to change your attitude and good things will happen."

"So my run of bad luck is all my fault? *I* killed my mother's roses and turned my dad into playboy of the month with my negative attitude?" She rolled her eyes. "Who knew I had that kind of power?"

"Scoff if you want, but people have known about the power of positive thinking for years."

So now Gloria was channeling Norman Vincent Peal? Lucy sighed. Her best friend meant well, and maybe it wouldn't hurt to listen to her. "Okay, okay. So how do I achieve this attitude adjustment?"

Gloria grinned. "I know just the place. There's a new dance club on Montrose. We can go there Wednesday night. It's ladies' night."

So Wednesday night found the two friends at *Stayin' Alive,* a three-story homage to disco fever. Disco balls cast dizzying spirals of light on the dance floor, which pulsed with colored strobes in synch with the music. Hundreds of twenty-somethings dressed in polyester leisure suits, bell-bottom cords and slinky nylon shirts gyrated on the dance floor or cruised among the club's three bars in search of the perfect dance groove, the perfect partner or maybe just the perfect cosmopolitan.

"Isn't this place wild?" Gloria shouted over the throb of a synthesizer and did a dance turn in the three square feet of space the two friends had staked out near the second floor bar.

"Wild," Lucy agreed. She sipped the too-sweet *Pink Thing* the bartender had assured her was the house specialty and watched a man in platform moon boots and a massive Afro dance with a girl in a patchwork skirt and peasant blouse. Usually she had no trouble getting caught up in the energy of a place like this, but tonight it all seemed so...well, *desperate.*

"See anybody you know?" Gloria spoke right into Lucy's ear so she wouldn't have to shout.

She shook her head. "I think I saw someone from my old job, but she danced by so fast, I couldn't be sure."

"Marla from the crisis center is here. And one of Dennis's buddies, Simon."

"Why didn't Dennis come with you tonight?"

"I told him he couldn't." She linked her arm with Lucy's. "This is a girls' night out."

Lucy nodded. She supposed a girls' night out was better than no night out at all. Her conscience reminded her that she could have accepted Greg's dinner invitation. She told her conscience to shut up and took another sip of the too-sweet drink.

"Oh my God! Is that who I think it is?"

She followed Gloria's pointing finger toward the other end of the bar, where a lanky man with spiked black hair and leather pants stood talking to a pair of bleached blondes. Something about the guy *was* familiar. Something about all that leather...

Her mouth dropped open. "I don't believe it! That's Xavier." The artist she'd dated a couple of years ago. The baddest of the bad boys she'd ever gone out with. They'd drifted apart after her mother got so sick.

"At least he's not wearing a leisure suit," Gloria said. "I never did understand what you saw in him."

Seeing him now, she wondered a little herself. He was too skinny, with pale skin and no real hint of muscles on his tattooed biceps. But he did have nice hair and a sort of swaggering, sexy walk. And a don't-give-a-damn attitude she'd always admired.

"Greg is much better looking," Gloria observed.

Lucy blinked. "We aren't talking about Greg."

"I'm just saying—he's much better looking than Xavier. Don't you think?"

"Well...yeah." She drained the last of her drink and set the empty glass on the bar. "But judging a person solely on the basis of looks is shallow."

"Xavier's the one who's shallow," Gloria said. "At least Greg has depth."

"Depth?" She faced her friend. "You met him once. What do you know about depth?"

Gloria's smile reminded Lucy of a cat. She looked so certain and pleased with herself. "I could tell a lot about him by the way he looked at you."

"Please! You're imagining things."

"No, I'm not. Greg really studies you. Like he wants to know everything about you."

"Oh sure. He thinks he already knows everything." She didn't want to discuss Greg right now. She was trying hard not to think of him at all, though he had an annoying habit of popping into her thoughts whenever she let down her guard.

She grabbed Gloria's arm. "Let's go over and say hi to Xavier." At least she hadn't embarrassed herself in front of him numerous times.

Adopting her best "woman of the world" expression, she led the way across the bar to Xavier and his entourage. He glanced up at their approach, then did a double take. "Luscious Lucy, is that you?"

She grinned at the sound of her old nickname. Okay, so maybe it was a little over the top, but at least it made her special. "Hey Xavier. How's it going?"

"Stellar." He turned to the blondes, who were both telegraphing the equivalent of obscene gestures with their eyes. "This is Bountiful Bonnie and her sister, Delicious Delia."

So much for special. She gave the pair a weak smile and lied through her teeth. "Nice to meet you."

They continued to glare. She turned her attention back to Xavier. "What have you been up to lately?"

"I'm part owner of this place." He spread his arms wide. "What do you think?"

"Oh, it's very...exciting." Could it be the man she'd let get away was actually making a fortune for himself? It figured.

"It's more than exciting. It's the hottest new club in town." He grabbed her hand and pulled her toward the dance floor. "Come on. I've got to show you this."

He led her across the dance floor, through the gyrating dancers to the DJ booth against the wall. He raised a hand to the DJ posted behind the sound board. "Hey Zeke," he shouted. "After this song, let's have a game of Twister."

The DJ gave him a thumbs-up sign. Xavier grinned at Lucy. "Wait'll you see this."

"*Twister?*" She made a face. "The game we played as kids?"

"Exactly! It's part of the whole seventies theme. People love it!"

She vaguely remembered the game played with a mat printed with colored circles. Players followed directions dictated by a spinner to place their hands and feet on the mat until everyone was so tangled up they could only collapse in a fit of giggles. "You play Twister with all these people?" she asked.

"You'll see."

"All right everybody! Grab your main squeeze and claim your spot on the dance floor." The DJ's bass voice boomed over the speakers. "Limber up those limbs and get ready to get down! It's time for...Twister!"

Lights flashed and music faded in and out as the dance floor began to change. Colored circles appeared beneath the dancer's feet until a thirty-foot pattern of red, green, blue and yellow polka dots stretched across the room.

Laughing and shouting, people raced to claim a spot on the "game board."

"Come on, let's play." Xavier nudged Lucy onto the floor. She stood on the grid of circles, fighting a growing nervousness. She liked games as much as the next person, but wasn't this a little weird?

Those who weren't playing gathered around the edges of the dance floor to watch. She spotted Gloria, who had a fresh drink in her hand. She raised it in salute and grinned.

The DJ started up a psychedelic soundtrack. "Now we'll spin the magic spinner and see where the game will start. 'Round and 'round and 'round she goes. Where she stops... Right hand red!"

The shuffling of several hundred pairs of feet almost drowned out the music. Lucy stared at the red circle at her feet. It was a long way down there. And her skirt was very short.

"Come on, don't be a stick in the mud." Xavier looked up from his bent-over position. "Put your right hand on red."

She glanced around, at the other people playing. They were laughing and smiling, obviously having a great time. She remembered what Greg had said about her not being as wild as she thought she was. Well, showing her underwear to complete strangers was pretty wild. She bent over and slapped her hand on the red circle.

"Left foot blue!"

"Left hand green!"

"Right foot red!"

"Right hand yellow!"

As the DJ shouted out directions, music pulsated and a spotlight picked out people in the crowd. A video camera projected their images on a giant screen, while spectators hooted and laughed.

Before long, Lucy and Xavier were hopelessly entangled,

one of his legs wrapped around hers, one of his arms thrown across her back. She could feel cold air rushing up her skirt and was grateful she wasn't wearing a thong. At least the black bikinis she wore were new, and in this light, no one would notice her cellulite....

She shrieked and almost fell over as something hot and wet brushed against her neck. As she fought to regain her precarious balance, she realized it was Xavier's tongue. He was kissing her neck with all the enthusiasm of a hungry child trying to denude a cob of corn.

She elbowed him in the chest. "Stop it!"

"Why? That's what the game is all about." He moved lower, to nibble her collarbone. "Oh Lucy, you always were so luscious."

At that moment, the spotlight found them. She ducked her head, hoping no one would recognize her. She prayed her butt didn't look huge, hoisted in the air this way and that Xavier would have the decency to stop slobbering all over her. Her arms were cramping and the floor smelled like dirty feet. This was supposed to be fun?

"Left hand blue!"

Around her, people started to fall. She tried to straighten up and stand, but Xavier had her trapped, his leg wound too tightly around hers, the weight of his body holding her down. "Don't quit now," he said. "The winners get free drinks."

"I don't want a drink. Now let me go." She shoved against him.

He laughed and hugged her more tightly against him. "You don't really want to leave me, do you?"

That was it. Time to get serious. She let him have it with her elbow once more. With a grunt, he fell back, arms flailing, knocking her off balance. She collapsed in a heap and lay on the floor, staring at the toes of a pair of scuffed boots standing on a blue circle inches from her nose. A familiar voice spoke in her ear: "Lucy, do you need some help?"

STAYIN' ALIVE wasn't the kind of place Greg normally hung out in. He was more comfortable in a neighborhood pub, where you could actually have a conversation with someone or play a game of pool. But he'd promised himself he was going to work harder to develop his social life and this was supposed to be the hottest place in town, so it seemed like a good place to start.

So far, he'd had one beer and danced with a couple of women who'd seemed painfully dull. Or maybe he was the dull one. Already he wanted to go home.

When the DJ announced the Twister game, he headed for the door. Hip or not, this place obviously wasn't for him. But then he'd spotted a familiar figure on the edge of the dance floor.

Lucy was here? It figured. Fate seemed to keep throwing them together, though he hadn't yet decided if that was a good or a bad thing. After all, she'd made it pretty clear she had no interest in him outside of gardening. Which didn't mean he was ready to give up on her yet. He didn't like to give up on something he wanted, whether it was a particular landscaping contract or a woman.

She was talking with a guy in black leather. The sight of them together made his stomach churn. Was this the sort of man Lucy went for—this skinny, pale fashion plate?

He moved closer, drawn to the scene like a rubbernecker in traffic. When she bent over and slapped her hand on the red circle on the floor, his heart beat faster. He'd figured he'd gotten over the thrill of looking up a girl's skirt when he left junior high school, but apparently he was wrong.

He had to hand it to her—she was flexible. Which made him wonder what else she'd be good at. Things requiring flexibility. Not that he went in for swinging from the ceiling, but with the right woman...

His hands clenched into fists as Leather Boy began nibbling at her neck. He told himself he should leave—that it wasn't any of his business what she did with another man. But he remained frozen in place, unable to look away.

When she looked annoyed, he felt like shouting. He started closer, not sure what he intended to do. When she shoved the guy off her and ended up in a heap on the floor, he rushed forward without thinking.

"Lucy, do you need help?"

Her expression was disbelieving. She closed her eyes, opened them again. "Please tell me this isn't happening."

He offered to help her up. When she didn't move, he hooked his hands under her arms and pulled her upright. As soon as she was standing on her own two feet, she pushed him away. "I'm fine," she said and stalked away.

He followed, pushing his way through the crowd and catching up with her at the door. "Don't go," he said. "Let me buy you a drink."

She whirled and glared at him, eyes flashing. "Look, despite what you may think, I'm not some damsel in distress who always needs you rushing in to the rescue."

He started to argue, but the DJ was playing songs again, and the volume from the music and the dancers drowned out his voice. He grabbed her arm and dragged her out the door, into the parking lot. At least out here, the decibel level was tolerable. He let her go and they stood under the pinkish glow of a mercury vapor light. "Now we can talk." He faced her, his arms folded across his chest. "Are you saying I was just supposed to let you lie there in danger of being trampled?"

She frowned and scuffed the pavement with the toe of her sandal. "I wasn't being trampled. And the only thing hurt was my pride. I'd have gotten up on my own in a minute or two."

"Your leather-clad loverboy wasn't helping, that's for sure."

"Leather-clad loverboy?" She lifted her head, those green eyes of hers practically throwing off sparks. "Xavier is just a friend. And it's none of your business anyway."

"He was acting pretty friendly all right. Is that the kind of guy you go for? The skinny vampire type."

She bristled. "Xavier is an artist."

"And that excuses bad behavior? Come on, don't you think you deserve better?"

She crossed her arms over her chest. "I suppose you mean someone like you. Someone who's always rushing in to save me from myself."

He frowned. Okay, so maybe she could have looked after herself back there. "You can't expect me to stand by and do nothing when I keep seeing you in these...these predicaments."

"Why not?" She lifted her chin. "Everyone else does."

"And you think that's a good thing?" He shook his head. "You know, I appreciate that you're an independent woman and all, but there's nothing wrong with accepting a little help every now and then."

She looked away, catching her lower lip between her teeth. She had great lips, soft and pink. The kind of lips a man wanted to kiss. But he didn't think she'd react very well to him coming on to her right now. It might look like his assistance came with strings attached. And maybe that was exactly what she was trying to avoid by insisting so adamantly on looking out for herself. "Look." He softened his voice. "I don't think you're some helpless 'damsel' and I don't see myself as a knight in shining—or even tarnished—armor. I just want to be your friend. And friends help each other out."

She looked up through the veil of her lashes. "Just friends?"

"Yeah." He shoved his hands in his pockets. It was either that or reach for her.

She nodded. "Okay. I can do friends." She glanced over her shoulder. "I guess I'd better go back inside and find Gloria."

The bands around his chest loosened a notch. At least she hadn't mentioned finding Leather Boy. "You sure you'll be okay?"

She nodded. "What about you? Are you going to stick around a while?"

He was tempted, if only to have the chance to talk with her more. To figure out her weird combination of seeming competence and sometimes out-there actions. But maybe the best strategy for now was to back off. He shook his head. "I don't think I'm cut out for leisure suit land."

She laughed. "Isn't it horrible? I had no idea."

"What about you? Are you staying?"

"I don't think so. I'm getting a headache. As soon as I find Gloria, I think we'll go home."

"Okay. See ya." He backed away, toward the parking lot.

She smiled. "See ya. And Greg?"

He stopped, holding his breath, waiting. "Yeah?"

"Thanks. Even if I didn't need your help, it's nice to know you were there. Just in case."

He grinned. "Any time."

He was sure he looked like a goofball, staring at her with a big smile on his face like a besotted golden retriever. But there wasn't anything he could do about it. When she turned and went back inside, he sprinted across the parking lot toward his truck. He and Lucy weren't exactly best buddies now, but at least they'd declared a truce. It was a start.

8

Gardening forces the impatient to wait.

LUCY HAD NEVER had a guy friend before. Was it even possible? Sure, it was possible, but with a guy like Greg? A guy who turned her on in spite of the fact that he was so unlike every other man she'd dated?

Maybe she was attracted to him because he *was* so different. Instead of talking about friendship, maybe she should just kiss him and get it over with. The experience was bound to be less than thrilling and she could get on with her life, instead of wasting time wondering if Greg had some secret desire to buy a motorcycle or take up skydiving.

She'd spent most of her life rebelling against domestic conventions. The thought of being sucked into suburban ordinariness at this late date made her shudder.

She was contemplating all this when her cell phone rang. She checked caller ID and answered. "Hello, Gloria."

"Hey, what are you doing?"

"Working." She glanced around the tiny reception area of Genetic Futures. Except for two clients in the back, all was quiet now. "But I can talk for a little bit."

"I called to see how you're doing after last night."

"I'm fine. How are you?"

"I have a hell of a hangover." Gloria took a long slurp of chai. "But I'll survive. You sure you're okay?"

"I didn't drink that much, remember?"

"I don't remember much of anything, except you going into the parking lot with Greg. What happened out there between you two?"

She frowned. "Nothing." A big fat zero.

"Come on, you can tell me. Spill."

"Honestly, nothing happened."

"You sound disappointed."

"I don't know what I am." She began pulling apart a paper clip. "Confused, I guess."

"Face it, the guy likes you. I can tell."

"But if he was really interested in me, he'd have stayed at the club to talk some more, or to dance, wouldn't he? Instead, he walked off and left me."

"Maybe he thinks you don't like him. I mean, you haven't exactly given him any encouragement.

"I don't know if I want to encourage him." She tossed aside the straightened paperclip and picked up another one.

"Why not? He's good-looking. Nice. He seems reasonably intelligent and he's got a good job."

"Yes, but..."

"But what? And don't say he's not your type."

She paused long enough to nod goodbye to a client who was leaving. He grinned and not so subtly checked her out. She ducked her head, hiding a smile of her own. Honestly, guys were so transparent sometimes. Except Greg. She had yet to figure him out.

"And don't say Xavier is your type."

"I used to think so. Now I don't know." When she'd seen Xavier last night, she'd felt exactly nothing. How was it that a man she had once practically drooled over now made her yawn? Xavier's two main interests seemed to be extolling the virtues of the seventies and trying to make out with her. Sure, he still had the leather and tattoo thing going, but underneath the dark and dangerous facade, there wasn't much there. How had she missed this before?

"Maybe I'm just not interested in a relationship right now," she said. "I've got too many other things going on. Trying to find a job, worrying about my dad, my mother's garden."

"You worry too much. Which reminds me why I called. My women's empowerment group has a special guest speaker Friday night and I want you to come with me."

"A what?" She started in on another paper clip. "Gloria, I don't think—"

"No, this is exactly what you need. The speaker's going to talk all about finding our inner strength as women and learning to listen to the goddess within."

She sighed. She didn't want to spend an evening listening to chanting and breathing incense, but how could she say no to her best friend? "I should stay home with my dad," she said. "He and I have hardly talked since I moved in."

"You can talk some other time. And he'll probably have a date anyway. Come on, I've got two tickets. I can't very well ask Dennis to go."

She grinned. "Why not? He'd be a big hit."

The second client left, smiling and whistling. As soon as he was out the door, he lit up a cigarette. She choked back laughter.

"Lucy!"

"Okay, okay, I'll go. But this is the last time."

"You won't regret it. This may be exactly what you need to figure out what to do about Greg."

She was still pondering whether this was so when she

came home and found Greg's truck in the driveway that afternoon. She gripped the steering wheel and stared at the Polhemus Gardens logo on the truck and debated backing out again. She could call Gloria and see if she wanted to go for a drink. By the time she got home, Greg would be gone.

"Don't be stupid," she told herself, and climbed out of the car. After all, she and Greg were friends. She didn't have to avoid him.

Instead of going into the house, she went through the gate into the backyard. Greg was there, on his knees pruning rosebushes, his sleeveless T-shirt stretched across his muscular back as he reached forward to trim the canes. She smiled, and stood for a while admiring him. At least her bravery had rewarded her with this very fine view.

Millie was working, too, gathering up the canes Greg cut, carrying each one to a pile by the fence. When she saw Lucy, she let out an excited bark and bounded to her, pompom tail whipping the air.

"Hey there, sweetie." She knelt and smoothed the dog's curls. "Are you helping?"

"She's a big help." Greg stood and came toward her, clippers in hand. "I never met a dog before with such a knack for gardening."

She scratched Millie's ears and was rewarded with even more enthusiastic tail wagging. "She's pretty special. I can't believe I never had a dog before. It's good to come home to such a warm welcome."

"Tough day?" He laid the clippers on the patio table and wiped sweat from his face with a towel.

"Not too bad, I guess." She stood and brushed off her skirt. "Just not very exciting."

"No more penguin costumes?"

She laughed and joined him in the shade of the patio. "No. Just receptionist work today."

"Where at?"

She couldn't believe the annoying rush of warmth to her face, but there it was. So much for appearing cool and sophisticated. Could she blame it on her mother's redhead genes? "Would you believe a sperm bank?"

He choked back laughter and she joined in. It was pretty ridiculous. "You're kidding?"

She shook her head.

"So, uh, do people come in and like, make donations?"

A fresh wave of laughter overtook her as she remembered how happy and well, *satisfied* the "clients" had always looked when they left the office. "Let's just say I didn't shake anyone's hand when they left."

They both lost it after that, giving in to belly-shaking laughter. He patted her shoulder and then they both sank onto a chaise longue. She stretched out her legs in front of her and he sat on the side of the lounger, their hips almost touching. She was aware of his nearness. He smelled like sunshine, loam and a not unpleasant hint of male sweat. The scent of a man who'd been working outdoors. She decided she liked it.

"So how's the garden?" she asked. Millie hopped into her lap and she began stroking her fingers through the dog's fur.

"I've been doing some more pruning and fertilizing."

He looked toward the forlorn bushes lining the back fence. To Lucy's eyes, they didn't look much better than they had a week ago when she'd discovered the damage. "Do you think they'll recover?"

He shook his head. "It may be too late for some of the bushes, but I'm hoping a few will survive. We may not know for sure until next year."

Disappointment settled like bricks on her shoulders. "Mom would be so sad to see them like this."

"Next spring you can plant new bushes."

She shook her head. "It wouldn't be the same. She chose each one of these roses herself. This was her special place. I wanted to make it right again. For her." But she hadn't been able to do it. She couldn't help feeling she'd let her mom down.

"I still have a few things I want to try," he said. "What about you? Do you go back to the sperm bank tomorrow?"

Speaking of letting her mom down... "No, tomorrow I'm the Cheezy Wheezy lady at Todd's Supermarket."

She couldn't blame him for his incredulous look. "Cheezy Wheezy?"

"Yeah, I squirt this canned cheese onto crackers and hand out samples." She shrugged. "It's not too bad. Of course, what I'd really like is a real job. Something I could stick with and make a career." That perfect life's work her mother had always assured her she'd find.

"What did you do before?"

"Different kinds of office work. I was an English major, so after graduation I landed a technical writing job. I was working for an online marketing company when I got laid off."

"Did you enjoy the work?"

"Yeah. I mean, I got to be creative, and since it was a small company, everything was pretty free-form. And I was good at my job." Maybe he'd believe her, maybe he wouldn't. She hadn't exactly given him much evidence of her competence to date.

He looked thoughtful. "So...would you say you're an organized person? Someone who could come into a place that was a mess and whip it into shape?"

She laughed. "Yeah, I could do that. As long as you don't ask me to cook, clean or grow anything, I can do pretty well."

He nodded and stared out toward the rosebushes. "How would you like to come to work for me?"

At first, she wasn't sure she'd heard him correctly. "What are you talking about?"

"I'm offering you a job. Come work for me."

There he went—rushing to her rescue again. Honestly, had she sounded so pathetic? "Haven't you been listening? I have no green thumb. I *kill* plants."

He shook his head. "This job wouldn't have anything to do directly with plants. I need someone to come in and organize my office, answer the phones and take care of paperwork. An office manager, I guess."

She narrowed her eyes, studying his face for any sign of pity or deception. But he continued to look at her with those clear brown eyes. Honest eyes. Eyes brimming with integrity, her mother's favorite quality in a man. "I appreciate the offer," she said. "But I really am looking for something I could make a career. I mean, I'm twenty-six years old. It's about time I decided what I want to be when I grow up."

His gaze swept over her and his eyes flashed with added warmth. "I could make some sexist comment about that, but I won't. Look, why not take the job for now? You can still look for a career, but this has to be better than another stint as Puffy the Penguin or the Cheesy Wheezy girl."

He had a point there. And steady work would allow her to pay down her credit cards and move back into a place of her own. "You're sure I wouldn't need to know anything about gardening?"

"I need someone to handle the computer inventory system, to keep track of the accounts and all that stuff. I can teach you what you need to know about plants and stuff. You're smart enough to pick it up quickly."

He thought she was smart? She couldn't keep back a

small smile. "You can say that after all the dumb predicaments you've found me in?"

"People only end up in situations like that when they're willing to stick their necks out. It's not a bad thing." He shifted on the chaise and avoided looking at her. "You make me think about taking a few more risks with my life. Maybe I'll even get a tattoo." He brushed his hand across the rose inked on the inside of her ankle. The feather touch sent a hot shiver through her, and she sucked in her breath and held it, waiting to see what he'd do next.

His eyes met hers. "Why a rose?"

She let her breath out slowly and pointed her toe, admiring the single bloom curving around her ankle bone. "I got it right after Mama's funeral. As sort of a tribute to her."

He nodded. "She was a special lady."

"Yeah. There was nothing she couldn't do—gardening, baking, sewing. She tried to teach me all the things she loved and I was a total klutz."

"But you can do other things." It was a statement, not a question.

She shrugged. "I'm okay with computers. Take me to a mall and I can pull together an outfit in half an hour. I made straight A's in English composition. But I'm not sure Mom saw the use in any of that."

"You're wrong there. I know she was proud of you. She talked about you all the time."

Her heart twisted a little at the words. "She did?"

He nodded. "Whenever I saw her at the nursery she'd have to tell me all about your latest job or your new apartment or whatever it was you were up to."

She nodded. That sounded like her mother, who'd devoted her life to her flowers and her daughter. "It's funny the things you miss about someone after they're gone, you know? I mean, you miss *them*, but when Mom was alive, I hated the way she was always telling me how to live my life. I never listened to any of her advice, and now that she's gone, sometimes I feel so...directionless. Like I'm still waiting for her to tell me what to do."

"Then I guess you have to draw on your memories of what she said."

She nodded. "It's silly, I guess, but I've been reading her garden planner. Here, let me show you." She reached into her tote bag and pulled out the little book she'd taken to carrying around with her. "She wrote all this stuff in here about gardening, but some of it, well, it could apply to life, you know? Listen to this." She opened the book and read. "Manure is messy and it smells, but putting up with the negatives now will result in a beautiful harvest in the future."

"That's really the truth," he said. "In life and in the garden."

She closed the book. "Makes me wish I'd paid more attention when she was alive. Maybe I'd have my life more on track now."

"My father always told me the best things in life could be found in the garden."

His voice was soft, his eyes searching hers, telegraphing some message she didn't want to decipher. She shifted on the chaise, creating more space between them. When she spoke again, her tone was businesslike. "So this job. How much does it pay?"

He straightened and assumed a more formal tone himself. "What did you make at your last job?"

She told him a figure. He didn't flinch. "We can start with that. Okay?"

"Any benefits?"

"Health insurance. 401K. Dental. And free gardening advice."

She laughed. "I guess I could use that. Okay. I'll take the job. And thanks."

"Great. Is Monday soon enough to start?"

"We've got a deal." She held her hand out to shake and he took it, then surprised her by leaning forward and kissing her cheek.

It was a sweet, tender gesture that nevertheless sent an excited tremor through her stomach. She stared at him, speechless. "What was that?"

He shrugged. "I felt like kissing you, I guess."

"Uh-huh." And that was all he could manage? "That wasn't much of a kiss."

His face reddened. "I was afraid you'd think I was out of line."

It figured. The man was so conventional. She leaned toward him, and lowered her voice to a sultry purr. "Why don't you try again and we'll see if I'm offended?"

She expected him to hesitate. Maybe even back down. She was bracing herself for disappointment when he pulled her close and proved that whatever his faults, bad technique was not one of them.

He started out slow, with a gentle but firm pressure, letting her warm up before he moved in for the kill. His arms wrapped around her, pulling her against his chest. She turned her head slightly, seeking closer contact. She could feel the sandpaper stubble of his beard, the iron-hard muscles in his shoulders and arms. *Mama mia,* but this was a kiss!

Heat washed over her and she let out a sigh. He took the opportunity to make a foray with his tongue, sending a fresh wave of giddiness through her. She wanted to cheer, to jump up and down and to blow raspberries at the part of her brain that had dared to think her physical attraction to this man was misplaced.

She also wanted to rip off her clothes and go after it right there on the patio lounger, but her conscience, or perhaps some shred of common sense implanted by her mother, put the brakes on that thought. She was going to be mature here. Less impetuous. A moan of regret escaped her, which he might have mistaken for passion. In any case, he tightened his hold on her and deepened the kiss.

By the time they finally broke apart, she was panting and dizzy. She stared at him, dazed. He grinned. "How was that?"

She tried to form her lips into a coherent sentence, but the only thing she could manage was "Wow."

Looking immensely satisfied with himself, he rose and gathered up the clippers and the towel. "There you go," he said, his eyes full of laughter. "You've got me taking risks already." He sauntered across the yard and out the gate, whistling under his breath. She was still staring after him, her heart pounding, when he got into his truck and drove away.

Millie's wet nose against her hand brought her out of her stupor. She looked down and could have sworn the little dog was smiling at her. "What just happened?" she asked.

Was she making a mistake agreeing to work for Greg?

Or was she finally doing something right with her life?

9

A man of words and not of deeds
Is like a garden full of weeds.

BY THE TIME Gloria picked her up to take her to the women's empowerment lecture, Lucy had rehearsed five different ways to tell her friend she was going to work for Greg Polhemus. She didn't want Gloria to jump to any conclusions. After all, this was just a job. Nothing more.

She wasn't sure what she was going to say about that goodbye kiss. Or if she'd say anything. She still didn't know what the kiss meant or what it would lead to next. It was as if Greg had lobbed a ball over the net into her court and it was up to her to decide whether to return it or not.

In any case, she didn't have a chance to say anything to Gloria right away. As soon as she opened the passenger door and slid into the car, Gloria said, "Thank God I had a good excuse to get out of the house. Dennis is acting so bizarre."

"Dennis? Bizarre?" She'd always figured Gloria had that adjective all wrapped up in that relationship. Dennis seemed downright straight-arrow in comparison. "What's he doing?"

"He didn't want me to go out tonight. He started whining about how I never stay home anymore. He said I have plenty of time for my friends and volunteer work, but none for him."

"You know we didn't have to go tonight on account of me," Lucy said. "I'd have been happy to stay home." In fact, she'd have preferred it. She'd been working up the nerve to talk to her father about his playboy lifestyle. She was close to finding the right words to voice her worries to him. Who knows, tonight might have been the night. Instead, she was facing two hours of mystic theory, strange chanting and weird smells—the hallmarks of any of Gloria's consciousness-raising activities.

If she was going to raise her consciousness, she'd just as soon do it in the shoe department of Dillard's, with a pair of Jimmy Choo sandals in each hand and the smell of Michael Kors perfume hanging in the air.

"That's not the point." Gloria clutched the steering wheel so hard Lucy thought she might rip it from the steering column. "The point is, I'm always so supportive of everything he does. All those nights in the comedy clubs. All those weekends at workshops. He should support me in my personal growth, too."

"Uh-huh." What else was she supposed to say? She was pretty sure Gloria wasn't referring to the expansion of her hips, but beyond that, personal growth was a mystery to her. "Maybe you could cut down on some of the volunteer stuff." Gloria did seem to be involved in a lot of "causes."

"The work I do is important!" The car swerved as Gloria turned to glare at Lucy. She faced forward again and steered back into her lane. "Besides, the only thing I'm involved in right now are the women's crisis center hotline, the dog park committee and COMA."

"COMA?" A group that represented unconscious people?

"The Chemical-free, Organic Metro Alliance. Our goal is to virtually eliminate the use of chemicals in Houston."

"Uh, Gloria? Houston's economy is pretty much based on the petrochemical industry. Not to mention we're the bug capital of the Southwest. If we didn't use gallons of bug repellent, the mosquitoes would carry us away. Don't you think you've picked a losing battle?"

"That's what everyone would like us to think, but we have the strength of our convictions behind us. We plan to target one major player at a time and convince them to pledge to eliminate the use of pesticides and destructive chemicals at all their facilities, as well as to introduce state-of-the-art antipollution measures. And we're asking them to commit funds to develop more organic alternatives to their products."

"You're asking them to spend money to put themselves out of business?" Lucy shook her head. "No one's going to do that."

"We're hoping to convince them it's the morally superior thing to do. Not to mention it will generate all kinds of good karma. People don't think about that kind of thing enough." She glanced at Lucy. "We've already made contact with our first targeted company."

"Oh. And who's the lucky winner?"

"Allen Industries. They're the parent corporation for a conglomerate of plastics manufacturers in the Ship Channel area. They have eight campuses on the Gulf Coast alone. Converting them to our cause will be a huge coup."

"And real chocolate that tastes great and is non-fattening would be terrific too, but that ain't gonna happen either."

"Go ahead and make fun. You and Dennis will change your minds when you see the kind of good real activism can accomplish."

"So Dennis didn't think much of the idea either?"

"He's only using his criticism to try to get me to back out of my commitment to the group." Lucy flinched as Gloria slapped the steering wheel. "The point is, I won't have him thinking he can manipulate me emotionally like this."

"Uh-huh." Whatever. She slumped in the seat and stared at the glow-in-the-dark St. Christopher statue on Gloria's dashboard. She was at the point in her life where she might actually appreciate having a man who wanted to spend his evenings with her. Just her and her guy. And Millie. A cozy little family.

Was that a sign of growing old? Or of growing up?

The women's empowerment group met above a women's studies book store. One look at the motley crew gathered for the class and Lucy decided a trip to the mall for a few lessons on dressing to impress would do more for their self-esteem than two hours spent listening to the overweight man with the Fu Manchu moustache and tie-dyed parachute pants who was introduced as the teacher of the class.

"Why is a *man* teaching about women's empowerment?" she asked Gloria as they took their seats on one of the sagging sofas arranged around the room.

"Shhh! Dr. Zerkowitz is an expert. He's written *Worshiping the Inner Goddess* and *Fulfillment With Fruit.*"

"Gee, if that's all it takes to be an expert, maybe I should write a book, too. Higher consciousness through shoe shopping."

Gloria gave her a sour look. What was wrong with Glor tonight? The fight with Dennis must be upsetting her more than Lucy had thought.

Dr. Zerkowitz sat cross-legged on top of a folding table and began speaking. "I want us to start with a centering meditation," he began, his voice the flat monotone of the airport recording that instructed *Please do not leave your baggage unattended at any time* ad infinitum.

Maybe I should take a trip, she thought as she closed her eyes. *A vacation from all my problems.* She tried to focus on her "inner light" as parachute pant man instructed, but the only image she could come up with was a big traffic light, stuck on yellow.

She hadn't slept well the night before, waiting for her dad to come in from his date, wondering about Greg...

"Now envision your spiritual guide walking toward you," the guru intoned.

She was surprised to see her mom, her red curls shaped into an awful poodle cut. What had she been thinking? Maybe this was the latest style on the other side, not that Barb Lake had ever cared much for fashion.

Her mom smiled, a big delighted smile that made Lucy smile, too. "I've found the perfect man for you," she said. She reached into the shadows and brought a man into the light.

Lucy gasped as she stared at Greg. But not exactly the Greg she knew. This one was dressed in his father's old coveralls and dirty baseball cap. He grinned and grabbed Lucy's hand. "Let's get hitched, darlin'," he drawled.

The next thing she knew, she was wearing her mom's old wedding dress, saying "I do," while her mother, dressed in a ridiculous cheerleading outfit, complete with blue and white pom-poms, jumped up and down and shouted "Yes! I knew I could get that girl straightened out!"

Dazed, Lucy drifted down the aisle with her new husband, who was still wearing those nasty coveralls. Then she had on her mother's old apron and three crying children clung to her while pots boiled over on the store. She looked out her kitchen window and watched as a gorgeous man on a motorcycle roared away.

"Wait for me!" she shouted, beating against the window. "Wait for me!"

She woke with a start to find herself stretched out on the old sofa with a dozen strange faces, and Gloria, staring down at her. Gloria was frowning. "Lucy, do you know you snore?"

She pushed herself up on her elbows and looked around. Zerkowitz was still sitting on the table, staring at her. "Apparently meditation sent you into an altered state," he said. "Tell us all what you saw during your breakthrough experience."

As if she would share that nightmare with anyone! "I...I think I'd better go now," she stammered, and scrambled to her feet.

Parachute pants stood also. "Don't be afraid to face your fears. In confronting our fears, we learn."

"Uh...no." She darted toward the door, dodging the outstretched arms of the other women. Spilling her guts in public definitely wasn't on tonight's menu.

She fled down the stairs and onto the sidewalk, where the humid night air didn't exactly revive her, but at least it was quiet out here. She paced up and down the sidewalk, fully awake now and fully annoyed. What was with her subconscious throwing up such a flipped out dream? What did it mean?

The door opened and Gloria joined her on the sidewalk. "What was that all about?"

Lucy shook her head. "I guess I'm not much for meditation. I fell asleep and had a weird dream."

"Want to talk about it?"

She shook her head. "Not right now. I don't think it meant anything anyway."

"Let's go over to Barnes and Noble and get some tea."

"Don't you want to stay for the rest of the meeting?"

She shook her head. "To tell you the truth, that guy is too weird even for me."

They laughed, and made their way to Gloria's car. Five minutes later they were enjoying grande chai lattes and browsing the aisles. "Let's check out the self-help section," Gloria said.

"I thought you already owned every self-help book written," Lucy said.

Gloria stuck her tongue out at her and plucked a volume off the shelf. "There's nothing wrong with wanting to learn from others," she said. "Maybe I'll find something here that will tell me what to do about Dennis."

"Maybe you should just stay home with him more," Lucy said. "You know, coddle him a little."

"He's a man, not a child. Besides, I want to know *why* he's doing this all of a sudden."

"Maybe he's feeling insecure, about his career or something, and he wants to know you're there for him."

Gloria stared at her. "What is with you tonight?"

"What do you mean?"

"You sound so...so logical. It's not like you."

Lucy shrugged and pulled a book off the shelf. "*Animal, Vegetable or Mineral—Find the Perfect Partner for You.* By Moonberry Grendal." Shaking her head, she slid the volume back in place. "*Make Peace With Your Past Lives,*" she read the next title. "Why don't they have anything really practical here? Written by an ordinary person."

"What do ordinary people know about life?" Gloria looked up from the volume she was studying.

"Lots. After all, we've lived it."

Gloria raised her eyebrows. "You know a lot about life? That must be why you're so together."

Lucy delivered a one-finger salute and the two friends gave in to laughter. "I'm sorry, but you left yourself so open for that remark," Gloria said. She replaced the book on the shelf and put her arm around Lucy. "But you know I love you."

"I know. And you're right. My life is not together. But it will be. One day."

Gloria led the way over to a pair of overstuffed chairs and sank into one. "So what's up with you and Greg lately? Have you seen him?"

She nodded. "He was working at the house when I got home yesterday."

"And?" Gloria leaned forward, her expression eager.

"And..." Lucy began breaking tiny pieces off the rim of her cup. "I'm going to work for him."

"Get out!"

She nodded. "He hired me as his office manager. It was too good an opportunity to pass up."

"No kidding. This is so perfect. You'll see him every day." She sipped her tea and grinned at Lucy over the cup. "You can really get to know him. See what develops."

"Right." One thing for certain, she was going to find out, somehow, what had happened to those old coveralls and that hat. If Greg confessed to wearing them, all bets were off.

WHEN SHE REPORTED for work at Polhemus Gardens Monday morning, Lucy felt as if a whole flock of butterflies had taken up residence in her stomach. Starting a new job was bad enough, without adding her confused feelings about Greg and her career prospects, or lack thereof, into the mix.

"Good morning." An older Latina woman greeted her when she walked into the nursery office. "May I help you?"

"Oh, uh, yes. I'm the new office manager. Lucy Lake." She offered her hand.

Deep dimples formed on either side of the woman's

mouth when she smiled. She took Lucy's hands in both of hers. "Lucy! So nice to meet you. I'm Marisel Luna, one of the horticulturists."

"Nice to meet you, Marisel." She followed the older woman behind the counter.

"You can put your purse in that filing cabinet there and I'll bring you some coffee. Greg should be here any minute."

The butterflies in her stomach started up again. She wasn't sure if she was ready to see Greg just yet. On one hand, you couldn't kiss a man like that and not acknowledge there was something going on between the two of you. On the other, her track record with the opposite sex didn't bode well for diving into a new relationship. Especially one that came with a job attached.

Aaargh! Why did she always end up in such impossible situations? Other people managed careers and boyfriends and their own apartments and even parents with hardly any trouble at all. Then here she was, feeling like she was juggling bowling balls and feathers while balanced on a unicycle.

The man himself walked in about that time and she started to stand up, but had to sit down again when her wobbly knees refused to support her. But he didn't seem to notice, since his eyes were focused on a bundle of mail in his hands. "Good morning, Lucy," he said, staring at a junk mail envelope as if it held the secrets to eternal happiness. "Are you ready to get to work?"

"No, I just showed up to goof off." She hated when people talked to her without looking at her.

"That's good. I'll show you the phone system and where everything is and the rest you can probably figure out on your own."

She picked up a pad of work orders that was lying on the

NO POSTAGE
NECESSARY
IF MAILED
IN THE
UNITED STATES

BUSINESS REPLY MAIL
FIRST-CLASS MAIL   PERMIT NO. 717-003   BUFFALO, NY

POSTAGE WILL BE PAID BY ADDRESSEE

HARLEQUIN READER SERVICE
3010 WALDEN AVE
PO BOX 1867
BUFFALO NY 14240-9952

Get FREE BOOKS and a FREE GIFT when you play the...

LAS VEGAS
GAME

Just scratch off the gold box with a coin. Then check below to see the gifts you get!

YES! I have scratched off the gold Box. Please send me my **2 FREE BOOKS** and **gift for which I qualify.** I understand that I am under no obligation to purchase any books as explained on the back of this card.

331 HDL DVCH   131 HDL DVCN

FIRST NAME

LAST NAME

ADDRESS

APT.#

CITY

STATE/PROV.

ZIP/POSTAL CODE

(H-F-02/04)

7	7	7	Worth TWO FREE BOOKS plus a BONUS Mystery Gift!
🍒	🍒	🍒	Worth TWO FREE BOOKS!
🔔	🔔	☘	TRY AGAIN!

Visit us online at
www.eHarlequin.com

counter and debated throwing it at him. "Are you talking to me or to that envelope?" she demanded.

He raised his head and met her gaze at last. "Huh?"

"I just told you I came here to goof off and you said that was fine. You obviously weren't listening to me."

"Oh. Yeah." He looked away again. Had he been in the sun or were his cheeks red because he was actually *blushing*? She moved out from behind the counter.

"If I'm going to work here, we ought to get a few things straight," she said.

"Sure." He picked up a ceramic toad, then set it down again. "What do you need to know?"

She moved closer, fighting nerves. She needed to know where she stood with him, but she couldn't bring herself to come right out and say that. "What time is lunch?" she blurted.

"Lunch?" His brows drew together in a frown. "Twelve. Twelve-thirty. Whenever you like. Marisel can watch the phones and front desk while you're out, so work it out with her."

"Okay." She gripped the front edge of the counter, still searching for words. "And when is payday?"

"Every Friday." He was still frowning, and he'd raised his head to look at her now.

She nodded and took a deep breath. Okay. Time for the big question. "And...uh...what was with that kiss the other day at my house?"

His cheeks were definitely redder now. He started to look away again, but she grabbed his hand. "Don't ignore me. I want to know what's going on."

He shook her off and took a step back. "Nothing's going on. I was out of line to do that. Especially with you coming to work here. I just...it was nothing." He turned and walked away.

She stared after him. Nothing. He called that nothing? The man was either a lousy liar or more uptight than she thought. And the prize goes to the answer behind door number two! Who was she kidding? Greg Polhemus's picture was next to the word "uptight" in the dictionary. What was worse, he didn't even see anything wrong with that! "You know what your problem is?" she blurted.

He stopped halfway to the door and raised his head. "What?"

"You always do the right thing. Or what you think is the right thing. If it isn't written down in the rule book in your head, you can't do it."

He turned to face her again. "I don't know what you're talking about."

"Yes you do." She glanced around them, at the rows of pots and plants and gardening tools. "Look at this. Your father expected you to come to work for him, so you did, right? And when he died, you took over the business, just the way he wanted. And you're still living in the house you grew up in, right? I'll bet it's still decorated the way it was when you were a little boy."

His frown deepened to a scowl. "So?"

"So why are you so afraid of stepping out of the lines?" She crossed the distance between them and prodded him in the chest. "Would it kill you to risk your dignity and unbend a little bit? Act on impulse?"

"I suppose that's your specialty? Acting on impulse? Without considering the consequences?"

"Everything we do has consequences," she said. "And not all the unexpected ones are bad. At least I know how to have fun."

"So you think I'm boring?"

"Yes."

"Then that kiss was boring."

"No."

"Make up your mind. I'm either boring or I'm not."

"You're boring. But you have potential."

His laughter startled her. "Glad to hear you think I have potential." He glanced over her shoulder and his smile faded. "Look, this is a little awkward, what with you working for me and all. I don't want people thinking I'm taking advantage of you."

"As long as I don't think so, what does it matter what anybody else thinks?"

He gave her a long look. Heat spread through her, clear down to her toes. Maybe there were other problems about combining a job and romance that she hadn't considered. For instance, what did you do when thoughts of getting it on with your boss distracted you from your work?

"Maybe we'd better talk more about this later," he said. "I have work to do." He turned and walked out. She picked up a flower pot and hefted it in her hand. If she'd known she would definitely miss his head, she might have risked throwing it. Just as a kind of editorial statement.

She felt a warm hand on her shoulder. "He is just like his father that way. So quick to regret acting on impulse."

She turned and found Marisel looking at her with kind eyes. "How long have you been standing there?"

Marisel set the mug of coffee she'd brought on the counter. "Long enough to hear that he kissed you and now he thinks he shouldn't have."

She shrugged and moved back behind the counter. "Do you think he's right? If we're going to be working together, maybe we shouldn't make things complicated."

To her amazement, Marisel laughed. "Oh *niña!*" she said, shaking with mirth. "What happens between men and women is not as complicated as people think. When two people are meant for one another, it just...happens."

She held out both hands, open at her sides. "I have seen it many times." She leaned over and patted Lucy's shoulder. "Don't you worry. If it is meant to be, he will be kissing you again. He won't be able to stop himself."

She stared at the older woman, wondering why such an impossible load of baloney made her feel so strange. Everyone knew romance didn't just happen. The whole relationship game took study and strategy and *work*. All that waiting around for love to "just happen" got you was a bunch of Saturday nights home alone and a refrigerator full of frozen dinners for one.

"Ah, you young people are so cynical." Marisel joined Lucy behind the counter, her voice good-natured. "But when you're older, you'll see that I'm right."

She couldn't help but smile at the words. How many times had her mother said the same thing? *Someday, you'll appreciate my advice* she'd say.

Right now, her mother would probably tell her to get to work and quit letting a man mess with her head. She turned to Marisel with a smile. "Would you show me how everything works around here?"

"Of course!" She laughed again. "Everything but the boss man." She shook her head. "Him you'll have to figure out by yourself. But I think that will be a fun job for a woman like you, no?"

Fun. Lucy wasn't sure she'd have used that word. But interesting. It was bound to be interesting....

10

Sometimes even our best efforts yield only weeds.

GREG TOLD HIMSELF he didn't have time to worry about Lucy right now. He needed to concentrate on his meeting with the Facilities Manager for Allen Industries' corporate headquarters. He'd worked for weeks on his presentation and he couldn't afford to blow it because he was distracted by the most fascinating and frustrating woman he'd ever met.

This contract would make him a major player in the landscaping business. His father had gone after Allen Industries for years and had failed every time. With his typical stoicism, he'd shrugged off his disappointment with "Ah, well, we have enough business anyway."

Enough for what? When Greg had taken over Polhemus Gardens, he'd immediately set his sights on winning the one thing that had always eluded his father. When he'd looked over his portfolio one last time before putting it in the mail, he'd been confident he had the contract nailed. He'd never done better work.

Now, sitting in a waiting room in the thirty-story steel-and-glass headquarters of Allen Industries, his confidence wavered. He was running with the big dogs here. Was he ready for this?

"Mr. Davidson will see you now." A secretary in an ice-cream pink suit escorted him down a carpeted hallway to a large office. Smoked glass on two sides of the room afforded a view of Tranquility Park. An older man with a fleshy face and receding brown hair looked up from behind a massive walnut desk. "Good morning, Mr. Polhemus."

"Mr. Davidson." Greg shook the man's hand. "Thank you for seeing me."

"Please, sit down." Davidson gestured to a leather desk chair.

Greg sat, crossed his legs, then uncrossed them. "Mr. Davidson, I—"

"I've taken a look at your portfolio." The older man cut him off.

"Yes?" He waited, holding his breath.

"Very impressive. Especially for such a small concern."

"Our small size allows us to give individual attention to each client." He'd rehearsed the phrase so often it was a wonder he didn't mumble it in his sleep.

Davidson nodded, his expression bland. "That is, of course, something we would expect."

He leaned forward. "I'm confident we can provide the design sophistication you're looking for, while maintaining a landscape that is both low-maintenance and environmentally friendly."

A deep vee formed between Davidson's brows. "You're not one of those eco-fanatics, are you?"

"Uh, no. Of course not." Was this some sort of test?

"We've had problems in that area before. Some extremists hear 'plastics' or 'manufacturer' and automatically assume we're out to poison the planet."

"The program I've outlined in my proposal would stand up well to criticism from environmentalists," Greg said. "In addition, lessening the reliance on chemical fertilizers and pest control is more cost effective."

Davidson sat back, hands folded on his stomach. "Tell me something about yourself, Mr. Polhemus. What are your hobbies and interests?"

He shifted in his chair. "Uh, I enjoy gardening, of course. Sports." Not that he had time to play any. He searched for something else to add and found nothing. When had he become so dull?

"Any church or political affiliations?"

He shook his head.

"Are you married?"

"No, I—"

Davidson leaned forward. "Are you seeing someone? Living with someone?"

"Uh, no." He sat up straighter. "Excuse me, but what does that have to do with this job?"

Davidson's smile didn't reach his eyes. "Allen Industries feels strongly about upholding family values. We prefer to work with others who embrace the same ideals. In fact, if we were to decide to hire you, we would require you to allow us to conduct a background check. In these days when the press is eager to expand upon any hint of corporate scandal, we feel we can't be too cautious."

"Uh, right." The words almost stuck in his throat. What kind of place was this? "I have nothing to hide." His life was too boring for even good gossip.

Davidson nodded and closed the portfolio. "We'll be making our decision in the next couple of weeks. Someone will call you."

"Thank you. I'd just like to—"

"Diane will show you to the lobby."

The woman in the pink suit was back in the doorway. As he followed her back to the lobby, disappointment sat like a rock in his chest. He hadn't had the chance to point out the more unique features of his proposal or list all the benefits of working with him as opposed to one of the bigger concerns. Had Davidson been interested in anything he had to say or was he merely being polite? Humoring him so that later, when he lost the bid, he couldn't make the claim that he hadn't been fairly considered for the job.

He could almost hear the old man: "Best to stick to what you know. Find your niche and stay with it. Let the work speak for itself. All that flash and fanciness isn't necessary if you concentrate on the basics—a job well done for customers who appreciate you."

What about customers like Allen Industries, that didn't appreciate him—yet? Why not go after people like them with the extra "flash and fanciness" they expected? Good work alone hadn't been enough to convince them to award a contract to his father all these years, so Greg had determined to try another approach. If it didn't work, did that really mean he was wrong?

Or had his dad been right all along? Was he better off staying the same, never branching out, remaining as boring as Lucy thought he was?

GREG THOUGHT about all this as he walked around his house that night, looking at the wallpaper that had been in place since he was in elementary school and the furniture that had sat in the same spots so long it had worn permanent grooves in the carpet. Lucy had never even been here before. How had she known?

He wandered into the bedroom and stared at the baseball trophies on the bookshelf and the faded Astros pennant on the wall. This wasn't a grown man's bedroom. It certainly wasn't the kind of place you could bring a woman.

He went out into the garage and returned with an empty box, into which he began tossing the trophies, the pennant and all the other things he'd accumulated over the years that had little to do with his life now. He should have done this a long time ago, but he'd been too busy working. He'd come home at night, heat up a frozen dinner and crash in front of the TV for an hour or so before falling into bed exhausted.

What kind of a life was that? Lately he'd wanted more. He cleared a stack of books from his bedside table and studied the titles. *The Ultimate Rose Book. The Rose Bible. Horticulture Guide to Common Garden Diseases and Their Treatment.* He'd consulted these books and others, searching for a miracle that would bring Barb Lake's rose garden back to life. Because that was what Lucy wanted from him.

And he wanted Lucy. Wanted her physically, but more than that, he wanted the flood of happiness that filled him whenever she smiled; the giddy, adrenaline rush her impulsiveness kindled in him and the warm feeling of protectiveness that overtook him whenever she was near.

He sat on the edge of the bed and stared at the box full of discards at his feet. Who would have thought one woman could make him feel so much, and leave him so confused? Sparks flew between them whenever they were together. When his gaze met hers, he would have sworn he read the same desire and longing in her eyes that he felt. And then she'd turn away, seemingly cool and unconcerned. Was that the way all women acted or Lucy's own method of driving him to distraction?

"So what are you going to do about it?" He spoke out loud, as if the bare shelves and blank walls might answer. He was met with silence, and yet, in his head, he heard his father speaking. *If you want something, son, you have to work for it.*

He knew about work, all right. Knew too much about it. Maybe it was time to stop concentrating so much on the business and put the same kind of effort into his personal life. A smile stole over him as the idea took root. He'd study Lucy Lake the way he'd studied her mother's roses. He'd woo her and wow her and he wouldn't take no for an answer. He'd show her just how good one ordinary man and an extraordinary woman could be together.

LUCY HAD every intention of turning the Polhemus Gardens office into a model of efficiency, simultaneously wowing Greg with her organizational skills and demonstrating that she could be as professional and job-focused as he was.

Unfortunately, her hunky boss, or rather, thoughts of him, kept interfering with her work. She'd be sorting through customer files and have a sudden image of him in her backyard, shirt stretched tight across the muscles of his back as he trimmed the rosebushes. Or she'd pick up an invoice and her lips would tingle with the memory of that surprising kiss.

What was really going on between the two of them? She'd been sure he wasn't her type, but then he'd kissed her and now he was practically all she could think about. What was up with that?

Could she really be falling for such a clean-cut, upstanding, *ordinary* guy? Was it a sign of desperation or was something else at work?

One thing she knew for certain: that hadn't been an ordinary kiss. Like Snow White awakened from her long sleep by the prince, her dormant sex drive had been sent into hyperalert by the touch of Greg's lips.

So what happened now? If he'd been one of her usual bad boys, she could be pretty sure he'd try to get her into bed. She'd pretend to resist, but before long she'd give in. They'd have a good time and see where things led from there. She'd learned not to expect too much formality or commitment from the dark and dangerous sort. It was frustrating sometimes, but she'd been sure that when she found the *right* man, things would be different between them. He'd *want* to be with her instead of always riding off into the sunset alone, so to speak.

Of course, that hadn't happened yet. So maybe it was time to give a different sort of man a chance. But what did a "good" guy like Greg want from her? Did he see them going out a few times, hanging out together as a couple? Would he eventually want her to cook dinner for the two of them? Would he bring her his shirts to iron?

Those were the kinds of things ordinary people did when they got serious about each other, weren't they? That was what her mom had done. Even liberated Gloria had been known to iron for Dennis, and when they'd first moved in together, she'd made it a point to learn to cook all his favorite foods. Would Greg expect that of Lucy?

The thought made her queasy.

She took a deep breath. Okay. No need to panic. She was attracted to the guy. But no need to rush into anything. She had plenty of time to decide what she was going to do.

She glanced at the clock—11:45. Close enough. "Marisel, I think I'll go to lunch now." She grabbed up her purse and headed for the door.

The older woman looked up from pruning a potted shrub. "Where were you planning to go? If you like subs, the place on the corner makes really good ones."

"I'll have to try that some other time. Today I thought I'd go to the mall. Get in a little shopping." Nothing like a half hour trying on shoes to make her feel like a new woman. With a new pair of sandals, she might even be prepared to take the next step with Greg. Whatever that turned out to be.

GREG ALMOST COLLIDED with Lucy in the doorway of the shop when he returned from lunch that afternoon. He stepped back to let her enter ahead of him, and she gave him a half smile before she darted toward her desk. Marisel looked up from the computer and smiled. "Did you find anything nice at the mall?" she asked.

"A few things." Lucy glanced at Greg, then hurried behind the counter.

"What did you buy?" Marisel asked.

"Um, nothing much." Why was she looking at him like that? As if she was guilty of something she didn't want him to know about. "Just odds and ends."

"What kinds of odds and ends? Any good bargains?" Marisel was relentless.

Greg decided to play along. He leaned on the counter. "Yeah, what *did* you buy?" The way she was blushing, he figured she'd stocked up on underwear or sexy lingerie, a thought that set his heart beating double time.

She blushed bright red and he had to bite the inside of his cheek to keep from laughing out loud. Had to be underwear.

"I...um, I bought a set of cookware."

"Cookware?" What did a woman like Lucy want with cookware?

"What kind?" Marisel apparently found nothing odd about the purchase.

"Um, stainless." Lucy turned to the older woman. "It was on sale and well, I don't have a good set." She shrugged. "I thought it would be a good investment."

"I thought you didn't cook," Greg said.

She frowned at him. "Maybe I'll take a class."

"I guess I'll take my own lunch now. See you two in an hour." Marisel waved as she passed on her way out the door, leaving Greg truly alone with Lucy for the first time since the kiss that had rocked his world.

He watched as she stowed her purse and settled in front of the computer, ignoring him. Oh no, he wasn't going to let her get away with that. "How are things going?" he asked, walking around the front counter and standing next to her chair.

"Uh. Okay." She looked up from the stack of folders she'd been rifling through. "Everything's a mess. Did you know that?"

"That's why I hired you." *That and the fact that having you around makes my work anything but routine.* He leaned against the desk next to her. "Can you straighten it out?"

"Eventually. I've almost got all the outstanding invoices entered into the computer. I'll start on the inventory next."

"I've been so busy with everything else, I guess I let the paperwork fall behind." He'd let his whole life fall behind, but no more.

"I'll say. You've probably lost money and don't even realize it." She turned back to the computer and began entering a string of data.

He studied her, his gaze settling on the back of her neck. He liked the way her dark hair curled against her pale skin. It made her look so delicate. Fragile even, like an exotic flower that had to be pampered and coddled. Of course, she was anything but. A person had to be tough to weather the trials and indignities she'd suffered and still come out smiling.

"What are you grinning about?"

Apparently, she'd been watching him, too. Their eyes met and his grin widened. "I was just remembering the first day I met you, when Kopetsky tossed you out of your apartment."

She frowned. "I don't see what's so amusing about that."

"No, No." He rushed to explain himself. "It wasn't that you were being evicted—it was the way you stood up to Kopetsky. You were down, but you weren't out. I like that about you."

Her eyes widened. "You do?"

"Yeah. No matter what, you're never boring or predictable."

She flushed. "About yesterday. I shouldn't have said all those things."

"No, it's okay. You're right."

She stared at him, her surprise evident. "You mean you're not mad at me?"

He shook his head. "I've even been thinking I should make some changes. I might even redecorate my house. That is, if I can find someone to help me."

She grinned. "I might have a few ideas."

"I was counting on it."

Their eyes met and held, heat arcing between them. He thought of ideas he'd like to share with her, ideas about the two of them, together. Alone. Possibly naked...

As if reading his thoughts, her cheeks flushed deep pink. She jerked her gaze away from him, feigning great interest in a display of plant stakes across from them. "This is a great place you have here. Everyone seems to like working here. Marisel was telling me some of your employees have been here twenty years."

Or maybe she was blushing because she'd had a few ideas of her own about them. The smile he gave her was anything but innocent, though his words were. "I think gardening gets in some people's blood."

She avoided his eyes and tapped a pencil against the desktop. "I don't guess it made it into mine."

"Right now I'm just as glad you're better with paperwork than plants." He nodded toward the computer.

"You're going to save my bacon. Maybe you should think about becoming an accountant or something."

She made a face. "I may be good with numbers, but that doesn't mean I want to spend my life with them. I'm looking for something a little more...creative."

"Yeah, you do strike me as the creative type." *Maybe we could be creative together.*

She either didn't catch his innuendo or chose to ignore it. "Maybe it's hopeless. Maybe there's no such thing as the perfect job." She gathered up the scattered files and stacked them neatly. "In any case, this definitely beats dressing up as a penguin or answering phones at the sperm bank."

"I don't know, I thought you were pretty cute in that penguin costume." *Hey, she was a babe in anything.*

She stuck her tongue out at him. The childish gesture sent a ripple of happiness through him. Now, if he could only figure out a way to let her know how he felt, without scaring her off.

"Paychecks are due Friday, right? Do you write them out by hand or do you have a computer program?"

So she was back to business. Fine. He'd be patient. And persistent. "I have an outside service handle payroll. A courier will bring the checks in Friday morning. You'll need to put them in envelopes for each employee to pick up." He opened a drawer and lifted out a box of envelopes, along with a box of fliers. "You'll also need to put one of these safety information sheets in each one."

She picked up one of the fliers. "This is all in Spanish."

"Almost all my employees are immigrants from Mexico and Central and South America. Even the ones who speak English don't read it that well. When I have information I want to make sure they understand, I give it to them in Spanish."

She replaced the flier in the box. "I guess I can relate. I

took Spanish in high school, but not enough to really get along if I had to live there."

"A lot of the workers would like to learn better English and to study to apply for citizenship, but they don't have the time—or the money—for night school."

"You should offer classes here, after work. They could attend one or two nights a week."

He nodded. "Good idea. But who would I find to teach? It's not like I can afford to pay a lot."

"I could do it."

He blinked. "You? I mean, not that I don't think you could, but why would you?"

Her smile made him feel light-headed. "I have a degree in English. And I took some education classes. It would be a good way for me to use at least a little of what I learned in college. And besides, I'd enjoy helping them."

And it would mean they could spend more time together, after work. "Great. When would you like to start?"

She glanced at the desk calendar. "Next week? Monday? Would that be enough time for people to plan to attend?"

"I think so. I mean, if it's right here and it's free..."

"I can print up a flyer tomorrow to put in all the paychecks." She caught her lower lip between her teeth. "Do you think you could help me with the Spanish?"

"I'll be glad to." He pulled up a chair and sat next to her. "Tell me what you want to say and I'll translate."

They sat side by side at the desk, heads together, focused on the computer screen. But every cell in Greg's body was aware of the woman next to him: of the way she chewed her lip when she was thinking, of the scent of herbal shampoo and fabric softener that teased his nose every time he leaned close, of the pink lip gloss slicked across lips he very much wanted to kiss again.

They were still hard at work when Marisel returned from

lunch. "I see you two are friends again," she said as she passed them.

"Of course we're friends." He narrowed his eyes at the woman who was like a second mother to him. What did she know? Had Lucy said something to her?

"That's good. I like to see young people be good friends." She giggled and moved on out the door toward the greenhouses.

"What's with her?" Lucy asked.

He shook his head. "I should have warned you. Marisel thinks she's not doing her job if she doesn't have her nose in everyone's lives."

"I don't mind. She's really sweet. And she means well. She sort of reminds me of my mom. You know, full of advice I have no intention of following."

"Yeah, it's best to just smile and nod and go on doing things the way you would have anyway."

"Exactly!" Her eyes were bright. "Still, it's amazing how much they say sticks with you. To this day I feel self-conscious if I wear white shoes before Memorial Day because Mom said it simply wasn't done."

He laughed. "I know what you mean. My dad planted sweet peas on St. Patrick's Day, no matter what the weather forecast, so I always do that, too."

"I guess we're our parents' children, no matter how much we try to be different, huh?"

"Yeah, but we're our own people too. Every generation adds its own quirks, I guess."

"Yeah." Their gazes met for a long, awkward moment. *What is she thinking?* he wondered as he studied his own reflection in her deep green eyes. He wished they weren't at work. He'd kiss her again. Right on that luscious mouth.

She was the first to look away, though the way she licked her lips, he wondered if she'd been thinking the same thing he had. "So, when were you thinking of redecorating?" she asked.

He blinked. "Redecorating?"

"You said you wanted me to help you fix up your house."

"Oh. Yeah. I do."

"So, is this something you wanted to do right away?"

"Yes. Why not?" If she was going to help him, she'd have to come to his house. They'd spend time alone. Anything could happen... "What are you doing Saturday?"

"I don't have any plans. Why don't you come by my house and pick me up and we'll see what we can do."

Oh, yes. They'd see what they could do. Such an innocent phrase that opened up all kinds of possibilities. In the meantime, maybe he'd better clean house. And change the sheets. Just in case.

11

In even the most beautiful gardens, you have to put up with a few bugs.

LUCY WAS EATING breakfast Saturday morning and leafing through a stack of design magazines that had belonged her mother. She'd pulled out the magazines hoping to come up with a few ideas for Greg's house.

She already had plenty of ideas of things to do with Greg, most of which involved taking all their clothes off and finding out how far this amazing physical attraction they shared would take them.

She hugged her arms across her chest and fought back a shiver of anticipation. Or maybe fear. With her track record with men, the second emotion might be more sensible.

She sat up straighter and turned the page. Fine. She was starting a new chapter in her approach to relationships. From now on, slow and easy was her motto. If something was real, it would last. If it didn't...well, at least she could *try* to avoid being hurt.

"Morning, sweetie." Her dad shuffled into the kitchen in his stocking feet and bent to kiss her check. "You're looking pretty this morning. You remind me of your mother, wearing her dress like that."

She glanced down at the blue flowered sundress she'd pulled from her closet that morning. "This dress isn't

Mom's. It's mine." At least she was pretty sure it was. One of the problems with a serious shopping hobby was difficulty keeping up with acquisitions.

Dad shook his head. "No, it was your mother's. She bought it a few months before she died. It was one of her favorites. Nice to see somebody getting some use out of her things."

She leaned over and sniffed the dress. White Shoulders engulfed her. She felt dizzy. Disoriented. What was she doing wearing her mother's dress?

Oh God, it was happening! Other people had predicted it and she'd laughed at them. But here she was, turning into her mother. The next thing she knew, she'd look in the mirror one morning and find herself putting on blue eyeshadow and Peach Sunset lipstick. She'd be overcome with the urge to make homemade noodles or organize the attic. She'd start wearing practical shoes and carrying a packet of tissues and two quarters taped to an index card in her purse. She'd tell anyone who asked that the quarters were for a pay phone if she lost her cell phone or the battery died. Never mind the fact that you hardly ever saw a pay phone anymore. Or that all the times previously when her mother had given her quarters taped to cards, she'd used them to buy Diet Cokes. (Hey, people's ideas of emergencies were different, okay?)

"How are you this morning?" Her father's question pulled her from her musings.

"I'm fine, too." Except for the whole turning into her mother thing. But she wasn't going to think about that. She'd think about the wonderful evening ahead of her. All the diets she'd been on proved she was an optimist, so maybe this thing with Greg would work out differently. Better not jinx it by talking about it just yet, though.

Her father's relationships, however, were something she

was perfectly willing to talk about. "What did you do last night?" she asked.

He stirred creamer into his coffee and popped two slices of bread into the toaster. "I had dinner at a place called Leon's. You ever been there?"

She shook her head. "What kind of food?"

"I thought it would be Italian, because the only Leon I ever knew was Leon Santini. But turns out it was French." He made a face. "Little bitty servings of food that looked more like art than something you'd eat."

She tried to picture her father, whose favorite eatery up till now was Al's Rib Shack, eating French food. "How did you end up there?"

"Oh, Jeannie wanted to go there."

The sudden queasiness in her stomach had nothing to do with the Lucky Charms she'd had for breakfast. "Who's Jeannie?"

"One of the secretaries at the Union Hall. Nice enough gal."

I'm sure she's nice to you, Lucy thought. *That doesn't mean she isn't a conniving witch looking for a sugar daddy.* "Have you been dating her long?"

"Nah. We only went out this one time." He took butter and jam out of the refrigerator.

"Um, how old is she?" She clutched the edge of the table as she waited for his answer.

"Oh, I don't know. Maybe thirty? When you get to be my age, they all look so young."

She wet her lips. No way could she keep quiet any longer. She only hoped he wouldn't take this wrong. Men might have muscles and brawn and all that going on, but their egos might as well be made of spun sugar. And no matter how old or ugly or impaired, they all seemed to have been born with the idea that they were irresistible to women. It figured they would get this and could stand up to pee, too.

"Daddy, why do you date so many young women?" she asked. "I mean, not that you aren't a nice-looking man, with a great personality but...well, what about someone closer to your own age?"

He chewed a bite of toast and stared off into space, his expression thoughtful. She found herself counting the bites as she waited for his answer. She was up to fifteen when he took another sip of coffee and said. "I guess I just meet a lot of young women. The only ones my age I know are all old friends of your mother. Dating them doesn't seem right, you know?"

She nodded. In a weird way, it did make sense.

He finished off his toast and carried his plate to the sink. "Don't worry, hon. I'm not getting carried away with any of this. I just figure this beats sitting at home alone in front of the boob tube."

"I'd stay home and do something with you," she said.

He smiled. "You're young! You should be out enjoying yourself, meeting other young people. Not sitting home baby-sitting your old man."

"No, Daddy. Honest. I really would like to spend more time with you."

He smiled. "If you're really serious, we'll make it a date. But you'll have to wait until next weekend. I'm booked up until then."

She was tempted to ask him his secret. How was it that in a few short weeks, her father had had more dates than she'd had in the past year? What did he have that she didn't? Besides a full wallet and ostrich skin cowboy boots.

She was still contemplating this when someone knocked on the back door. Millie was sleeping under the table and hadn't moved. "Some watchdog you are," she said as she went to answer the door.

She was surprised to see Greg waiting on the back steps. "Hey," he said.

The sound of that one word and the smile he gave her made her insides as gooshy as melted chocolate. Oh baby, did he do it to her. It was all she could do to keep herself from throwing her arms around his neck and kissing him until be begged to come up for air.

But she reminded herself she was going to take things slow. She would be calm and sensible and most of all, patient. Good things were worth waiting for, right?

She stepped back. "Good morning. Would you like to come in?"

"Sure. Cute dress. Is it new?"

"Um, not exactly."

He followed her into the kitchen. Millie woke and trotted over to greet him. He knelt and stroked the dog's soft fur. "I brought over some flats of annuals to set out in the front beds," he told Lucy.

"Oh gosh, I forgot all about those. I've been so worried about the roses." She looked over his shoulder, out the window overlooking the backyard. The bushes along the fence were still little more than bare twigs. She sighed. "It's hopeless, isn't it? They're not going to bloom again."

He joined her at the window. "We've done everything we can. Some of them might surprise us yet. Life is full of surprises." His eyes met hers, and she wondered if he was thinking about them, about the surprising way they'd gotten together. All her reminders to play it cool flew out the window and she was ready to move on to plan B—dragging him into the bedroom and ravaging him—when her father interrupted.

"I'd better get moving. I'm going to the track today and the first race starts at noon."

"Got a hot date?"

She sent Greg a dirty look for asking the question, but he ignored her. Her dad shook his head. "No date, but I might meet someone there. A lot of good-looking women come to the horse races. You'd be surprised."

When they were alone, she felt safe in looking at Greg. At least now if she were to spontaneously combust, she wouldn't give her father a heart attack.

He grinned at her. "So do you have some ideas for my house?"

She nodded. Oh yeah, she had ideas all right. She was thinking of showing him one right then when her father poked his head into the kitchen again. "Have you see my boot?"

"Huh?" She turned to him, her mind reluctant to leave fantasies of having her way with Greg.

"My boot. I can only find one of them." He held up a single cowboy boot.

"Uh, no. I haven't seen it. Maybe it got shoved under the bed or something."

"Maybe. I'll go look."

"Now, where were we?" She hooked her thumbs into Greg's belt loops and pulled him closer.

"What are you doing?" He was grinning and not exactly fighting her off.

"We're not at work today," she said. "And I was thinking about that kiss...."

"Yeah, I've been thinking about it, too." He leaned closer and she closed her eyes, anticipating his lips on hers.

"I found my boot." Her father came into the room again, a ragged cowboy boot in one hand, the toe chewed almost off. "Your dog has been chewing on it," he said accusingly.

Reluctantly, she pulled away from Greg. "My dog? She's your dog, too."

"Not if she destroys my favorite pair of boots. Now I'll have to wear the regular calfskin."

He stomped away and Millie moved out of the shadows to sit at Lucy's feet. She looked at the dog. "You should be ashamed of yourself."

Millie didn't look the least bit ashamed. If anything, she looked rather pleased with herself.

She knelt in front of the dog and rubbed behind one floppy ear. "What's gotten into you lately?" she asked. "Why are you destroying Dad's boots?"

"Maybe she needs a boyfriend." Greg came to stand behind her.

Lucy shook her head. "I don't think that's it. She's got a scar on her tummy that I think means she's spayed."

"Then maybe she's unhappy being here by herself all day. Why don't you bring her to work with you next week?"

"You mean it?" She smiled up at him.

"Sure. She can't hurt anything and she'd probably enjoy the company."

"Thanks. I'll do it."

They looked into each other's eyes so long, she was sure they really were about to kiss this time, but the chiming of the front doorbell put an end to that idea. "This better be good," she grumbled, hurrying toward the door, Greg and Millie at her heels. If this was another vacuum cleaner salesman or someone wanting to save her soul, they'd be saving up for dental work after she got through with them.

She checked the peephole and was stunned to see Gloria. She'd never seen her friend look so awful. She jerked open the door. "Gloria, what is it? What's wrong?"

Gloria looked at them mournfully. She had dark circles under her eyes and her face was pale. "Dennis and I had a terrible fight. I need to move in with you for a while."

12

Sometimes the best thing you can do is nothing.

RULE NUMBER SEVEN in the *Girlfriends Guidebook* states that when your gal pal has had a fight with her main squeeze, the former light of her life is now officially pond scum. However—and here is the point a lot of girlfriends overlook—you are not allowed to say this. You are only allowed to nod and make sympathetic noises when *she* says this. Otherwise, when the couple gets back together (as studies have shown will happen fully fifty percent of the time, more if he is either gorgeous or rich) she will remember every time you compared her lover boy to toenail fungus and your name will be scratched off the wedding guest list.

Considering that Lucy actually *liked* Dennis, she vowed to withhold all judgment. "Of course you can stay here," she said, opening the door wider. Millie danced at her feet, whimpering her distress. "Come right in."

"Thanks." Gloria glanced over her shoulder. "I have a few things in the car."

"I'll get them," Greg said, wisely deciding to stay as far in the background as possible until he could make a break for it.

While Greg went out to Gloria's car, Lucy led her friend into the kitchen. Millie trailed along and positioned herself under the table. "Would you like some coffee? I can make fresh."

Gloria slumped into a chair. "Do you have any herbal tea? I think I need something soothing."

"Uh, sure." She opened a cabinet and began rifling through boxes of artificial sweetener, jars of creamer and packets of throat lozenges. "I think we have some tea up here somewhere...." She spotted a box at the back and snagged it. "Um, it's PMS tea. I was feeling desperate one day and gave it a try."

"Did it help?"

She shrugged. "I don't know whether it was the tea or the half box of Dove bars I had with it." She studied the label. "But it's herbal and it's supposed to relieve stress."

Gloria waved her hand. "I'll try it. It couldn't make me feel any worse."

The front door opened and Greg called to them. "What should I do with the dogs?"

At the mention of dogs, Millie let out a low growl. Lucy looked at Gloria. "You brought the dogs?"

"I couldn't just leave Sand and Sable with *him*. He'd probably go off to some audition and forget all about the poor darlings. Not to mention that he didn't really want to adopt them in the first place. He wanted a German shepherd until I pointed out to him the dire plight of retired racing greyhounds. Can you believe I actually had to convince him of our moral duty to adopt them?"

"Imagine that." It was a bad sign when the friend who's come to you for comfort won't even speak the ex's name.

"So you don't mind if they stay here? They're wonderful dogs, especially since Sable's skin condition cleared up."

"Uh, sure, it's okay." *What skin condition and is it contagious?* "That'll be fine. For a few days."

She finished putting the kettle on and sat across from

Gloria. Millie immediately climbed into her lap. "What happened? What did he do?"

"He said I cared more about the plight of strangers than I do about him!" Tears welled in her eyes and she buried her head in her hands and sobbed.

"There, there. It'll be all right." She stood and came around to rub her friend's shoulders.

"He doesn't appreciate how hard I work to make this world a better place. He thinks everything should be about *him*. As if my attending his comedy performances is more important than helping Albanian refugees find affordable housing!"

Lucy nodded, though she wasn't too sure *what* exactly she was agreeing with. "So he's upset because you missed a performance. Where was this?"

"At the Laugh Stop. As if he hasn't performed there a hundred times. And it's not like I haven't already heard all his jokes a hundred times. He practices before the mirror in our bedroom every single night. How many times am I supposed to hear the one about the one-legged accordion player and still think it's funny?" She buried her head in her arms again, loud dramatic sobs almost drowning out the sound of the tea kettle whistling.

Lucy was making the tea when Greg lumbered into the kitchen, bowed under by the weight of four bulging suitcases. "Where should I put these?"

She stared at the suitcases and began to feel woozy. "Uh, the spare bedroom is at the end of the hall, across from my room." She turned to Gloria. "How long do you think you'll need to stay here?"

"I don't know. I just couldn't bear to live in that house with him one more minute. I mean, he's so incredibly insensitive. How can he look at the statistics on global warming and not see that we have to do something right away?"

"Right." She wondered what exactly they were supposed to do, but was afraid to ask. It might involve wearing ugly shoes or doing without certain essential beauty products. Saving the planet was important, sure, but what difference did it make if you had to look like a hag to do it?

Her father came in, his hair wearing a fresh coat of Butch wax and his calfskin boots polished to a high shine. He looked at Gloria. "Hello there. You girls going shopping today?"

Gloria raised her head and sniffed. "Hello Mr. Lake. No, we're not going shopping. I'm too depressed to go shopping."

Lucy blinked. This was bad. This was very bad. She couldn't imagine being too depressed to shop. The day she found out her mother had cancer, she headed to the mall and spent four hundred dollars in three hours. A record even for her. It didn't make her feel better, but to her way of thinking it was better than crawling into bed and refusing to come out, which was the other option she'd considered. "Gloria's going to stay here for a few days," she said.

Her father nodded. "It'll be just like old times. A slumber party." He kissed Lucy's cheek. "You girls don't stay up too late. And keep the music to a reasonable level. Wish me luck at the track."

"Yeah. Good luck." She hoped he meant luck at the betting window, and not with one of the women who frequented the races.

"You're so lucky," Gloria said when Lucy's dad was gone. "Your father is such a nice man. Mine was a louse like...like...like *him!*" She began blubbering again, blowing her nose on a paper towel between sobs.

Greg reappeared in the doorway. "I put the suitcases in the bedroom and the dogs in the backyard."

"Thanks." She gave him what she hoped was an encouraging smile. *My friend is nuts sometimes, but that doesn't mean I am* she wanted to say.

"I can't believe after all I've done for him he would treat me this way!" Gloria wailed.

Greg took a step back. "Okay. Well, I'll just, uh, leave you two alone."

"I'll walk you to the car." Anything for a breather from Gloria's ranting and sobbing.

"Will she be okay?" he asked when they were safely outside.

"Yeah. She's always been a little, well, dramatic."

He glanced back toward the house. "Yeah." His eyes met hers again. "I guess we'll have to take a rain check on decorating."

"I guess so." Go to Greg's house and make out with him or stay home and listen to Gloria sob? Gee, some choice. Still, a friend in need and all that.... "We'll do it some other time, I promise."

"Okay. I'll leave the annuals on the front porch and take care of them later."

"Yeah, that'd be good." She'd forgotten all about the annuals. Their discussion about them seemed hours ago.

He kissed her then, a surprise move that delighted and touched her. She came this close to throwing her arms around him and begging him to take her somewhere far away. But at the last minute sanity prevailed—or maybe it was her mother's dress imbuing an extra measure of maturity. She stood on the curb and waved as he drove away, then went back in the house.

"I'm so upset I left the house without eating." Gloria stood in front of the open refrigerator. "Do you have any organic orange juice?"

"I think all we have is the regular kind. Frozen."

"Oh." She looked disappointed. "What about organic yogurt?"

Lucy shook her head. "I think there are a few hot dogs and some leftover Jell-O. Oh, and we have SpaghettiOs and Lucky Charms."

"SpaghettiOs? The ones with the little meatballs?"

"Yeah. They're not organic, but..."

Gloria chewed her lip, then nodded. "I suppose it wouldn't hurt this once...." She picked up her purse and slung it over one shoulder. "I think I'll go lie down for a little bit. Call me when it's ready."

"Sure. You know where your room is. I think the bed's even made." The sheets weren't organic cotton and they'd probably been washed with a commercial fabric softener, but she didn't think now was the time to point that out. Maybe later, if it looked like Gloria intended to move in permanently.

When Gloria had shut the bedroom door behind her, quiet descended on the house like fog rolling in. Lucy put the SpaghettiOs on to heat, then sat at the table. Millie leaped into her lap again. If Mom were alive today, she'd know what to do with and for Gloria. She'd have some wise method of handling Greg, too. And Lucy's father wouldn't be a problem at all. He'd be mowing the lawn or down at the hardware store buying nails for some fix-up project her mother had devised.

She idly petted the dog and stared at the untouched cup of tea across from her. "Be glad you're a dog," she said. "Life's probably a lot simpler for you, huh?"

Millie licked her chin and wagged her tail. Lucy hugged her tight. It wasn't the same as talking to Mom, but it did help. She reached across the table and picked up the mug of tea. PMS was a week away, but she'd take all the antistress potions she could find. Though frankly, she didn't think herbs were enough to handle the tension she was feeling. Maybe vodka would do it...half a bottle or so.

BY MONDAY MORNING, in her efforts to keep from snapping at Gloria, Lucy had ruined a manicure and ground her teeth until her jaw felt like she'd been sucker-punched. The quirkiness she'd always found so endearing when viewed from the distance of mere friendship grated in the proximity of becoming roommates. This must be what happened in some marriages: the way someone laughed or left her shoes in the living room never much figures into the dating portion of a relationship. But face that laugh and those shoes every day of your life and you developed nervous twitches and began to entertain fantasies of shoving the shoes down the laugher's throat next time you had to listen to that hee-haw.

In Gloria's case, her insistence on organic foods and the Zen chanting she began at 6:00 a.m. had Lucy ready to scream. Then there were the dogs. Sand and Sable had taken over the living room, sleeping on the couch and scattering chew toys all over the rug. When she caught Sable eating all of Millie's food while Millie watched with a wounded look on her face, she could barely control her rage as she dragged the dog away and locked her in Gloria's bedroom. The two friends had had a terrible fight about it, Gloria accusing Lucy of mistreating the stressed-out dog.

Stressed out? By Monday Lucy felt like the poster child for stressed out. She would have done anything—including wearing that horrendous penguin costume again—to escape another day spent discussing the merits of macrobiotic versus vegan diets and all the ways wearing clothes from the GAP was bad.

When Gloria announced she planned to work from home

this week—or rather, Lucy's home—Lucy knew she had one more reason to thank Greg for her job at the nursery. Millie seemed grateful to get out of the house as well. She was waiting by the car when Lucy came out that morning, though how she'd gotten out was anyone's guess. When they arrived at work, Millie scampered into the office and greeted Marisel with much tail wagging and excited yips.

"Isn't she a cutie!" Marisel bent to scratch the dog's ears. "What's her name?"

"Millie. I hope you don't mind. Greg said I could bring her to work."

"Why would I mind? I love animals and a little dog like this wouldn't bother anyone, would she?"

"She's really very well behaved." She stashed her purse in the filing cabinet and booted up the computer. "Whoever had her before I did must have trained her well."

"So you have not always had her?"

"No. She just showed up one day." She glanced at the dog, who was strolling the aisles, checking out the displays of plants. "I don't know what I'd do without her now."

"She likes plants." Marisel clapped her hands together as the dog trotted down the aisles. "What a smart dog."

Lucy laughed. "She does like plants. Go figure." She sat at the computer and called up the inventory database. "I think I'll get caught up on this inventory today. Then I can take a look at the billing system. I have a feeling it's a mess, too."

"Before you start that, there's something you have to see." Marisel opened a drawer and pulled out a sheet of notebook paper. "Look at all the people who signed up for your class tonight."

She took the list and read the scribbled name. She counted twelve, including Marisel. "You're attending? But you speak beautiful English. And I know you read it, too."

"I thought maybe I could help you. You know, translate and things like that." She shrugged. "Besides, what else am I going to do on a Monday night?"

"Don't you have family? Or someone to go home to?"

Marisel shook her head. "My Eduardo died ten years ago now and my sons are grown and living in Brownsville. Usually I go home and watch television, but I thought this class would be fun."

"I'd love to have you help me," Lucy said. "Actually, I'm relieved. My Spanish is a little rusty and I was afraid I might not be able to understand everyone."

"I thought I could help you with that."

Both women looked up as Greg entered the office. Millie ran to greet him. He scooped up the little dog and patted her side. "I see our little mascot is here and ready to go to work."

Lucy laughed. "She'll make a great mascot. She can be the official greeter."

He set the dog on the floor again and picked up the class list. "Are these the people who've signed up for class?"

"So far," Marisel said. "Others will probably show up at the last minute."

Greg looked at Lucy. "Are you ready?"

She took a deep breath. "I'm a little nervous, but I think I'm ready. I copied out some of the gardening wisdom from my mom's garden planner for everyone to practice with. I wanted something that would be a little familiar to them."

"That sounds good." He leaned on the counter. "I hope you don't mind if I stick around to listen in."

On one hand, the thought of having her boss listen in on her first-ever go at teaching made her stomach do backflips. But the thought of her potential *boyfriend* being there to support her kindled definite warm fuzzies. She smiled. "That would be great."

A woman who had a business caring for office plants came in and Marisel went to help her. Greg moved around the counter. "So how are things with Gloria? Is she still at your house?"

Lucy nodded. "She's driving me bonkers. I mean, I knew she was always a little...eccentric...but now I think she's downright weird."

"What does she do that's so weird?"

"We don't have recycling pickup in our neighborhood, but she refuses to throw away a can or bottle. So she rinses them out and leaves them all sitting on the counter. My refrigerator is full of all kinds of weird-looking stuff like kelp paste and sprouted wheat nuts. And she gets up at six o'clock in the morning and goes out in the backyard and starts chanting. I mean, this is not how I want to wake up in the morning."

He made a face. "Maybe you can send that somewhere and win a prize. 'My weirdest friendship.'"

She laughed. "Maybe so. At least it might make me feel better."

"Maybe she and Dennis will patch it up soon and she'll go home."

"I hope so. But I don't know. I'm beginning to really sympathize with Dennis."

Not to mention seeing Gloria and Dennis's relationship fall apart made her a little panicky. If two people she'd thought were so perfect for one another couldn't get along, it didn't bode well for her own budding romance with a man who was so different from her, did it?

13

Be prepared for surprises—you may plant petunias and end up with squash, and vice-versa.

AT SIX THAT EVENING, Greg began moving plants and hauling chairs into the nursery's retail space to create a makeshift classroom. Shortly thereafter, workers began filing in. Marisel introduced each one, most of the names familiar to Lucy from her organizing of the payroll records.

"This is Fernando, from Guatemala. Luis from Mexico. Arturo is from Honduras. Jésus from Mexico, Calvino from Mexico also, Sebastian from Venezuela, Irmina and Jacinta from Mexico, Kesara from Colombia, Monica from Honduras and Nalda from Mexico."

Lucy stood before her students, fighting panic. Why had she ever agreed to do this? These people had traveled long distances and probably endured a lot of hardship to get to this place and *she* was going to teach *them*? She stood there, a queasy smile on her face, and forgot everything she'd intended to say.

Greg stood and once more came to her rescue. "This is Lucy Lake," he said. "Some of you already know she's the new office manager. She's agreed to help you all improve your English."

"And I'm hoping to benefit by improving my Spanish." There. She'd finally remembered part of the speech she'd rehearsed last night. She smiled at Greg, to let him know she had things under control now. She took out her mother's garden planner and held it up. "Some of you probably knew my mother, Barb Lake. She collected a lot of gardening wisdom in her planner. One of the things I hope to do in this class is help you use English for practical things you'll need it for in your everyday life. Maybe we'll even take some field trips to a supermarket or the mall. Or to a library. I thought we'd start tonight by looking at some of the sayings and advice my mother wrote down about gardening, a subject I know you're all familiar with. Then maybe we can work together to add to Mom's collection."

Marisel had agreed to translate Lucy's words into Spanish, so she waited now while the older woman did this. Lucy opened her mother's journal. "The first saying or proverb is 'the sun does not shine equally on all gardens.' Would someone in the class like to tell me what that would be in Spanish?"

One of the younger women, Jacinta, raised her hand and Lucy called on her. *"El sol no brilla igualmente en todas yardas."*

"That's like a *dicho* we have," Jésus said. *"Bonito es ver llover aunque uno no tenga milpa."* He looked at Marisel. "I don't know how to say in English."

"It is beautiful to see the rainfall, even if we don't own a farm," she translated.

Lucy nodded. "That's great. What are some other gardening proverbs you know?"

For the next forty-five minutes, they discussed proverbs and their translations. Lucy pointed out similarities and differences in the two languages and answered the students' questions. From there, they moved on to good ways to learn another language. "I watch a lot of TV," Sebastian shyly volunteered.

"Soap operas!" Irmina grinned. "Like our *telenovellas*."

"Only *telenovellas* are better," Jacinta said. "More exciting."

"Magazines," Calvino said. "I look at pictures and try to read words."

"What about books?" Lucy asked. "Do any of you read books?"

The students looked at each other. Several shook their heads.

"I heard that Harry Potter book was good," Luis said. "But it's big, and expensive."

"My sister reads romance novels." Kesara giggled. "She says they're even better than *telenovellas*."

"In a few weeks, we'll go to the library and you can all check out books on my card," Lucy said. "Reading books will really help you improve your English. And I agree with Kesara's sister. Some books are even better than *telenovellas*."

"Where else can we go to study?" Arturo asked. "You said the mall. How about the movies?"

"I'd like to go someplace to learn more about your culture," Lucy said.

"Which culture?"

At the puzzled look on her face, the class laughed.

"We're from all different places," Fernando explained. "We all speak Spanish, but customs and traditions and even food for a person from Mexico aren't the same as for someone from Honduras or Guatemala." He grinned. "Anglos think we're all alike, but they got it wrong."

She flushed. "I guess I never thought about it that way." She studied their faces. At least they didn't seem to resent her ignorance. "What do you all think we should do?"

Rapid discussion followed, most of it in Spanish. Lucy was soon lost. Finally, Luis stuck up his hand and she called on him. "We've decided the thing we should do is take you to a Latin dance club."

The others nodded. "At *La Luna Y El Sol* on Wednesday nights at 6:30 they give free dance lessons."

"And they have a free taco buffet for happy hour," Arturo added.

Lucy laughed. "Then it sounds perfect. When should we go?"

"This Wednesday," Luis said. He looked at Greg. "If the boss man will let us off a little early to get cleaned up."

"I have to look *muy guapo* for the ladies," Jésus said, and slicked back his hair.

Greg nodded. "Okay. We'll quit at four on Wednesday, then everyone meet back here to go to the club."

"Do you know how to dance?" Lucy asked him.

He shook his head. "I figure we can learn together." His eyes met hers and a giddy wave of happiness shot through her at the thought of dancing with him.

"So are we done with class now?"

Irmina's words made her realize she'd forgotten she and Greg weren't alone. Blushing, she faced the class once more. "Yes. When you go home tonight or tomorrow, I want you to each write out three proverbs in Spanish and in English. Help each other if you get stuck or you can ask me."

There was a little good-natured grumbling over this homework, but most of the students were smiling and laughing when they left. "You did a very good job," Marisel told her on her way out. "You showed us all learning can be fun."

"I think it will be fun for me, too."

She stayed to help Greg put away chairs and move plants back into place. "I wish I'd thought of this years ago," he said. "But then, I couldn't have done it without you."

"You could have found someone else to teach." She set a ficus back in place and thought of the one her mother had given her so long ago. Mom would be proud of Lucy's teaching, she was sure. It was exactly the kind of productive activity her mom always tried to push Lucy into. She smiled. *It took a while, Mom, but see, I did listen to you all those years.*

"What are you smiling about?" Greg came up and slipped his arms around her.

"I was thinking about my mother. Sometimes when I read her garden planner, I feel like she's still here, giving me advice."

"Hmmm. What do you think Barb would have to say about you and me?"

There went her heart again, fluttering like a bird. "I think she'd approve," she said. "You're definitely her type."

He pulled her closer, and looked into her eyes. "What about you? Am I your type?"

Oh no. He wasn't going to get any kind of commitment out of her that easily. Men had spent years keeping her guessing. Now it was her turn. "I'm still deciding." She stood on tiptoe and wrapped her arms around his neck. "So you'd better be on your best behavior."

Before he could say anything else, she kissed him, effectively ending the discussion. This kind of communication was more fun anyway. Greg was a great kisser, a point definitely in his favor. He pulled her close and deepened the kiss, his tongue tangling with hers, sending her heart into overdrive. Oh yeah. Maybe Mom had been right. Maybe there was something to this integrity thing, if delivered in the right package.

THAT ONE KISS with Greg had evolved into an extended make out session behind the potted palms. The man might be straitlaced on the outside, but he was definitely uninhibited about sex. He had her panting and moaning in less than two minutes and she was ready to tear off his T-shirt and test the cushioning powers of the patio furniture when Millie's accusing stare brought them up short. "Why is she staring at us like that?" Lucy whispered in a brief respite when they'd come up for air.

Greg turned his head to look at the dog. She glared at them, not baring her teeth, but looking as if at any moment she might. "I don't know. Ignore her." He turned back to nibbling Lucy's neck.

She squirmed beneath him and pushed him away. "I can't do this with her watching us. It's too weird."

He kept nibbling her neck and began tracing a lazy figure eight around her nipple with one finger. "Pretend she isn't there."

The sensations rippling through her as he fondled her with fingers and tongue were almost enough to put the dog out of her mind.

Then Millie barked. Greg stilled. Lucy winced. "Maybe we should stick her in another room."

"Good idea." He shoved up into a sitting position and reached for the dog. Millie danced out of his way and barked again, her expression even more accusing.

Lucy giggled. "Maybe she thinks she's protecting me."

"Protecting you from what?"

"Well, you know." She gestured toward their half-naked bodies. "Maybe she thinks you're attacking me."

"Yeah, all that moaning probably did it. Maybe you should be quieter."

She might have held it together if he hadn't winked. Instead, she doubled over with laughter. "You haven't heard anything yet," she said. "Wait till you hear me scream. If you think you're man enough."

"The dog is going in the storeroom right now." He scrambled to his feet and reached for Millie again. She took off, racing around the counter, then back toward Lucy. Greg had to hold onto his undone pants with one hand, and lunge for the dog with the other. Just as he almost had her, she darted away. He stumbled over a display of plastic pots and lay there, his pants halfway to his knees, a pink plastic pot balanced on his head like a hat.

Shaking with laughter, Lucy sat up and pulled her shirt around her. "I don't think you're going to catch her."

"We can try to ignore her."

Millie barked and moved over between him and Lucy. Lucy's laughter subsided. "What are we going to do?"

He stood and zipped up his pants. "Maybe we'd better call it a night." The lust in the look he gave her now was tempered with tenderness. "Not that I don't want you, but I hadn't exactly planned for this to happen tonight. I don't have any, uh, protection with me. Do you?"

She shook her head. "No." That was the trouble with getting carried away by passion. It sounded romantic, but it wasn't very practical or smart.

She began buttoning her shirt. "I guess I'd better go home."

He nodded. "Yeah. I'm sorry."

"No, you don't have to apologize."

"Yeah well, believe me, tomorrow I'm going shopping."

"I'll be looking forward to it."

It was almost midnight when Lucy arrived home. She sat in the driveway for a while, remembering those moments of passion with Greg. They had been sweet, really. Frustrating, but sweet. Most of the tattooed bad boys she'd dated wouldn't have been that concerned about protection. It would have been up to her to put a stop to things and the evening would have ended on a sour note. Instead, she and Greg still had something to look forward to.

She tiptoed into the house, Millie at her heels. They passed Sand and Sable sacked out on the couch. She sighed. Might as well let sleeping dogs lie. She didn't want to wake her dad or Gloria and have to endure a grilling about where she'd been and what she'd been up to. As it was, they'd left the kitchen light on for her; there were sure to be questions in the morning.

When she got to the kitchen, however, she was surprised to find Gloria at the kitchen table, a bottle of organic wine open in front of her.

"What are you doing up so late?" She dropped her purse on the table and went to the cabinet to get a biscuit for Millie.

"I couldn't sleep." Gloria rested her chin in her hands, staring glumly into her wineglass. "Dennis called tonight. He said he had some mail for me but I really think he wanted to talk."

She took a glass from the cabinet and poured herself some wine, then sat next to Gloria. "How did he sound?"

"He sounded good." She glanced at Lucy. "You know, I've always loved his voice. All those years performing on stage—he enunciates so clearly."

Lucy drank the wine. Not the best stuff she'd ever have, but it would do. "What did you talk about?"

She sighed. "He asked about the dogs, then he asked how I was doing."

That was a good sign, wasn't it? "What did you tell him?"

Gloria sat up straighter and squared her shoulders. "That I was fine. I didn't want him to think I was falling apart without him or anything." She refilled her glass and took a long drink. "He said he had a gig at a new club in the Woodlands last night. He thought it went really well."

"Dennis is a really talented guy. He's in a tough business."

"He is funny. You know how I met him, don't you?"

"You took one of his classes, right?"

She nodded. "I got a speeding ticket and the judge said I could get it knocked off my record if I took defensive driving. So I looked in the phone book and saw the ad for comedy defensive driving and thought, why not?"

"Yeah, I took a class at the community center last time I got a ticket," Lucy said. "I swore I'd hit myself in the head with a hammer before I did that again. My class was two evening sessions and the second night I purposely wore shoes that pinched so I could stay awake."

Gloria smiled. "I sat up front in Dennis's class and he started picking on me right away, threatening to make me wear a dunce cap because my ticket was for speeding in a school zone. I heckled him right back and during the first break, he asked me out." Her smiled faded. "We've been together ever since."

The last words emerged as a sob. She lay her head on the table and Lucy patted her back. "Oh honey, you still love him, don't you?"

Gloria sniffed. "Of course I do."

"Then why don't you go back to him?"

She shook her head. "I can't until he apologizes. He said some terrible things. He said I was self-centered!"

There are times when truth between friends is good, but Lucy didn't think this was one of them. "Maybe the two of you should go to couples counseling. You know, learn how to communicate better. And maybe you could cut back a little on some of your volunteer activities and spend more time with him. I think the fact that he wants to be with you more means that he loves you very much."

Gloria rubbed at her eyes with a wrinkled handkerchief. "Maybe." Then she shook her head. "He'd never agree to it. He's so stubborn."

Said the queen of stubborn. But Lucy kept her mouth shut.

The back door opened and her father shuffled in. He stared at them in surprise. "What are you girls still doing up?"

"We were just talking." Lucy studied him. He had bags under his eyes and the lines around his mouth seemed deeper. "Where have you been?"

"I had a date." He went to the refrigerator and took out a carton of milk.

Another one? Was the man trying to set a record? "How did it go?" *And who was it with. What did you do?* But she was trying hard not to sound like an inquisitor.

He shook his head. "Not so good. Some of these young women are too demanding for me."

Lucy felt the hair rise up on the back of her neck. *What are they demanding? Tell me who this bitch is and I'll slap some sense into her.*

Her father poured a glass of milk and drained it. "I guess you have to keep getting out there if you're going to meet a good one." He set the glass aside. "I guess I'll go to bed now."

"Yeah, me, too." Gloria pushed out her chair and rose. "Good night."

"Good night."

Lucy sagged back in her chair. Two of the people she cared about most in the world were living here with her and both of them were miserable.

Millie hopped into her lap and nuzzled her hand. She

rubbed the dog's chin and looked into her sympathetic brown eyes. "I wish I could do something," she said softly.

What had Greg said? That you had to let people make their own mistakes? Not so easy when those mistakes moved in with you and set up house.

Besides, ignoring her father's and Gloria's unhappiness seemed too much like giving up on them. "I won't give up," she said out loud. After all, a woman who had faced down a hoard of sugar-crazed two-year-olds *and* survived the semi-annual Macy's shoe sale unscathed wasn't going to let a little thing like uncooperative relatives and friends get her down.

14

Achieving the results you want usually requires getting your hands dirty.

WHEN GREG WALKED into the office Wednesday afternoon, Marisel made a show of fanning herself. "Aren't you the handsome one," she said. "All the women will be fighting to dance with you tonight."

He flushed and looked down at the olive-green slacks and matching shirt and tie. "I asked Luis and he said this was kind of a fancy place we're going to." He looked at Marisel again. "Do you think it's too much?"

"Oh no." Marisel stood and slowly walked all around him. "You look very nice. Our Miss Lucy will be very pleased."

He straightened his tie. "Who said anything about Lucy?"

Marisel laughed. "Now is not the time to pretend indifference," she said. "Now is the time to be bold." She wagged her finger at him. "You are always too cautious, so much like your father."

"Being cautious isn't always a bad thing," he said. So far the risks he'd taken with Lucy hadn't gotten him much further along in their relationship. Yeah, she'd admitted she was attracted to him, that she liked him even. But she seemed unwilling to go much further than that. Even the other night, when they'd gotten so carried away, he'd sensed she was still holding back. Maybe it was time for him to back off a little and let her tell him what she wanted.

"Why do you look so glum?" Marisel asked.

"Where's Lucy?"

"She is in the ladies' room, changing clothes." She sat and patted the chair beside her. "Come here and tell me what's bothering you so."

Reluctantly, he sat in the chair, feeling a little like he had as a child when his father had sat him down for one of their "talks." Not a man given to long speeches, his father would invariably fall back on gardening analogies whenever he felt duty-bound to discuss weighty matters with his son. Thus, he'd learned of his mother's death as part of a long story about the life cycle of nature. His father's lecture on "the birds and the bees" had focused more on various winged creatures than the human equivalent. Fortunately, by the time the old man had gotten around to imparting this wisdom, Greg had already learned much of what he needed to know from various friends and purloined copies of *Playboy* magazine.

"Well?" Marisel prompted.

He rested his hands on his knees and stared at the polished toes of his shoes. "I guess it's obvious that I like Lucy. A lot. But I don't seem to be getting anywhere with her."

"Have you told her how you feel?" Marisel's face was kind.

"Yes. I mean, I've told her I want us to be together."

She clucked her tongue. "You've told her what you want. But do you know what she wants?"

He frowned. "I just told you, that's the problem. I don't know what she wants. I don't think *she* knows what she wants."

Marisel nodded. "In that case, you have to wait."

"You mean I back off and wait for her to make up her mind."

Deep dimples formed on either side of her mouth as she smiled. "You wait for her to make up her mind, but in the meantime, you help her. Show her what she'll be missing if she hesitates too long." She leaned closer. "You woo her. Do you know what I mean?"

"You mean I court her?"

She laughed again. "Not so formal as that." She tapped his hand. "Tonight, you dance with her. Tell her how beautiful she is. Look into her eyes. Touch her. Really listen when she speaks. Men don't do these things enough. Do this, and she will fall in love with you."

He stared at the older woman. She made it sound so easy. But Lucy was more complicated than that. Love was more complicated than that. Wasn't it? "I'll try," he said.

"Don't worry." Marisel patted his hand. "Like a fish, she is already on the hook. All you have to do is reel her in."

The tap of heels on tile announced Lucy's arrival from the back room. He rose as she rounded the corner and let out an appreciative whistle. Grinning, she paused and twirled around, the full skirt of her sleeveless dress floating around her. He had a tantalizing glimpse of her thighs before the folds of fabric settled around her again. She walked toward him. "I thought I deserved a new dress for dancing tonight."

"It looks great." He couldn't stop grinning. So much for playing hard to get.

"You look pretty sharp yourself." She reached up and tweaked his tie. "You clean up pretty nice."

"So are you ready to go dancing?" he asked.

"Yes, except I don't know what to do with Millie." Hearing her name, the little dog poked her head from around the side of the front counter.

"Why don't you bring her with us?" he said.

"To a club?" She looked doubtful. "They won't let her in."

"We'll sneak her in." Marisel held up her large straw purse. "She'll fit in here. She can hide under the table once we're there."

"I don't know," Lucy said. "What if she doesn't stay put? We could all be in trouble."

Marisel scooped the dog into her arms. "She and I have had a talk," she said. "I'm sure she will behave herself."

Greg laughed at Lucy's doubtful look. "You'd better listen to her. If Marisel told you to behave, wouldn't you?"

"All right." Lucy relaxed. "She can come with us." She gave the dog a stern look. "But if you don't behave, we'll lock you in the car."

The others began to filter in, dressed in their Sunday best, the women in brightly colored dresses, the men in fancy shirts and slacks. They looked like completely different people from the workers who labored for him every day.

"Are you ready to salsa?" Arturo asked, grabbing Marisel and executing a fancy dance step.

Lucy applauded him. "I'm ready. Though I can tell already you're all going to outdo me on the dance floor."

"Nah, you'll do fine," Arturo assured her. "The teachers at the club are very good. We'll have fun."

They split into groups and rode in several cars. Marisel, Millie and Lucy rode with Greg in his truck. To Greg's surprise, the dog made no protest about being stuffed into Marisel's bag. Maybe she really could communicate with the dog. She certainly seemed to understand *him* pretty well.

La Luna y El Sol occupied a hangarlike building on the east side of Houston. Inside, shimmering draperies disguised the metal walls and hundreds of faceted crystals hanging from the ceiling cast shards of colored light on the dance floor. A bar stretched the length of one end of the club, while a DJ booth overlooked the opposite end. Tables and chairs were clustered around the large dance floor in the middle of the building, where couples were already swaying and twirling to the seductive beat of salsa music.

They joined a dozen others who had arrived early for the dance lessons. An attractive young man and woman promised to have them all moving to the music before the night was over. "The rhythms of salsa music speak to our souls," the man declared. "Listen to your heart and you will not be able to keep from dancing."

For the next forty-five minutes, the students tried out various moves with each other and the instructors. To Greg's surprise, it was easier than it looked. As long as he remembered to watch Lucy and not think too much about how he looked, he could relax and enjoy himself.

Lucy was certainly enjoying herself. She would try even the most complicated moves, not caring if she flubbed them and laughing when the instructor told her that, as a *gringa*, she was handicapped, but that he thought she could overcome that and become a competent salsa dancer.

"Isn't this a blast?" she said, joining him by the bar when the lessons were over.

Her eyes shone and her cheeks were flushed with excitement. He smiled. "Yeah. It's great." He thought of the night he'd left her at the nightclub and gone home alone. What would have happened if he'd gone back inside with her that night?

He shook his head. No sense fretting about the past. Tonight he and Lucy were together and that's all that mattered. He took her hand. "Ready to try out a few moves on the dance floor?"

She twined her fingers with his. "I thought you'd never ask."

Of course, the first thing he did was step on her feet. He was ready to throw in the towel right then and suggest they sit down and have a drink, but she laughed and pulled him back into the crowd of dancers. "You're not a quitter," she said. "And neither am I. We can do this."

After that, it wasn't so hard. He'd never be Fred Astaire, but he managed to keep the rhythm and avoid crashing into other people. And there was something to be said for holding a beautiful woman in your arms, looking into her eyes and seeing happiness there.

He pulled her closer and she didn't protest. She shimmied against him, a provocative move. "Don't start a fire you can't put out," he warned.

"Oh, I can put it out." Her eyes teased him. "Did you go shopping?"

He grinned. "I did."

Her fingers trailed along his neck, tantalizing, promising deeper pleasures to come. "I can't wait. Do you think anyone would notice if we left now?"

"They'd probably notice. But do we care?"

She glanced around them. "I supposed we ought to stay for a little while longer." She smiled up at him once more. "Besides, I'm having fun."

He twirled her away from him, then back. There was something to be said for a slow seduction at that. He was about to tell her so when the smile melted from her face and she stumbled. He caught her. "What is it? What's wrong?"

She nodded over his shoulder. "You'll never guess who I just saw."

"Who?" *And who the hell would upset her so much?*

Her shoulders slumped. "My father."

"YOUR FATHER?" Lucy didn't blame Greg for his incredulous look. Her father, of the starched khakis and polished cowboy boots, was not the salsa-dancing type. She had known him to execute a stiff two-step or waltz at the occasional wedding or party, but as she watched him now attempting to swivel hips never made to swivel, she was embarrassed for him. The fact that his dance partner looked scarcely old enough to vote only made things worse.

"No, no. Don't look! I don't want him to see us." She buried her face against Greg's chest and his arms came around to pull her closer. The gesture made her feel so protected. So cared for.

"Do you want to go back to our table?" he asked.

She nodded and he steered them to the edge of the dance floor. From there, they retreated to the table. Greg flagged a passing waitress and ordered drinks while she searched the crowd until she spotted her father again. He'd given up really dancing by now, content to sort of shuffle in time to the music while the girl gyrated around him.

"Who is that with him?" Greg scooted his chair closer to her.

She shook her head. "I've never seen her before. Every time I turn around these days, he's with someone different." Maybe if he'd looked happy she wouldn't have this urge to jerk the woman off the dance floor by her long black hair and pluck out all her eyelashes. But her father had the pained look on his face of someone trying too hard.

"*Dios mio!* I haven't moved like that since I was a girl." Marisel sank into the chair on the other side of Lucy. "But why are you two young people sitting here? Why aren't you dancing?"

"We're taking a little break," Greg said. The waitress arrived with their drinks and he reached for his wallet.

Lucy sipped the *mojito* and stared glumly at her father

and his latest conquest. Marisel followed her gaze and raised her eyebrows. "Who is the handsome man you are staring at?" she asked.

"That's my father." She winced as he attempted a corkscrew turn, completely out of time with the music. "Dancing isn't really his thing."

"And who is the young lady with him?"

She sighed. "His date, I guess. I don't know her."

"Perhaps he met her here tonight and she asked him to dance," Marisel said.

"Maybe so." Not that it mattered. Her father was entitled to make a fool of himself any way he wished. But she didn't have to be happy about it.

"Grrrr."

Millie poked her head out of the straw bag under the table and looked out at the dancers. "And what are you complaining about down there?" Marisel reached down and gathered up the dog. "Are you ready to come out for a while?"

"Don't let the waitress see her," Greg said. "We'll all be thrown out."

"It's all right," Marisel said. "If anyone says anything, I'll pretend to be an ignorant old woman." She grinned, her dimples deep. "One of the advantages of growing older is that you can get away with amazing things as long as people think you're innocent and sweet."

Greg snorted. "Anyone who knew you would see through that bunch of bull."

She laughed. "People believe what they want to believe. And a lot of them think old people are harmless and brainless."

"You aren't that old!" Lucy protested.

"It's true I don't feel old, but to some of these youngsters—" She indicated the crowd of twenty-somethings around them. "To them, I'm practically ancient."

"My father's your age," Lucy said. "And he's a smart man. But lately, he hasn't been doing smart things."

As if to demonstrate, her dad attempted to dip his partner, almost dropping her. "He'll hurt his back," Lucy said. "What is he thinking?" But then, if she knew that, maybe she'd know why he was doing this desperate Don Juan act and she'd find a way to stop it.

"Grrrrr."

Millie growled again, her whole body stiff as she positively glared at Lucy's dad and his date. "Maybe we'd better take her outsi—"

She never finished the sentence. Millie leaped out of Marisel's lap, scattering glasses as she scrambled across the table. She landed in the middle of the dancers, somehow managing to avoid their feet.

Greg and Lucy weren't so lucky. They raced onto the dance floor too, and collided with half a dozen couples, who muttered curses and glared at them before reluctantly letting them pass.

Millie darted ahead, straight toward Lucy's father, who was back to shuffling in place, a dazed look on his face as if he, too, wondered what he was doing here.

Millie nipped at his partner's heels, effectively cutting her from the herd. Screaming, she stumbled back, crashing into a large man and his even larger wife. While the three of them shouted and gestured, Millie whirled to face Lucy's dad.

"Millie?" He looked around and spotted Lucy and Greg headed toward him. "What are you all doing here?"

But before they could answer, Millie made her move. With an angry bark, she leaped, and latched onto the meatiest part of Lucy's dad's anatomy. He let out a howl, and the people around them turned to stare at the older man with the irate poodle firmly attached to his rear end.

"I take it Millie doesn't approve," Greg said.

"You go girl," Lucy whispered, before wading in to retrieve the dog and escort her wounded father to a table.

15

*Gardening is like sex: we sometimes produce fine gardens,
but we mostly do it for other reasons.*

AFTER THE SECURITY GUARDS escorted them into the parking
lot of the club, Lucy finally spoke to her father. "Daddy, are
you hurt?"

He grimaced, holding both hands over the tear in his
trousers. "Only my pride." He looked down at Millie, who
sat at their feet, an innocent expression on her face. "I wonder what got into her?"

"I want to know what's gotten into *you*." Lucy folded her
arms across her chest and faced him. "What are you doing
here, and who is that woman you were with?" The woman
who hadn't bothered to leave the club with them, she could
have pointed out, but didn't. Frankly, it was in the chick's
best interest not to be around Lucy at the moment.

"I wish I had a good answer for you." He shook his head.
"Carmella seemed like such a nice girl and she made this
kind of dancing sound like so much fun. I figured what the
heck. I'll give it a try." He looked sheepish. "I guess it's not
something I'm cut out for."

"Where did you meet her?" Lucy asked.

"At the track. She was sitting next to me and we got to
talking." He shrugged. "It was just a friendly date, hon.
Nothing serious."

He looked so sad, she couldn't stay upset with him. She patted his shoulder. "I worry about you, Daddy. All this running around with younger women doesn't seem like you."

He sighed. "I know."

"Then why are you doing it?"

"I guess I'm just lonely. After a while, sitting around that house, without your mother there, got to be too hard."

"Oh, Daddy." Tears stung her eyes and she hugged him close.

"There you are, you naughty girl." Marisel exited the club and rushed toward them. She scooped Millie into her arms and hugged her close. "What were you thinking, biting the hand that feeds you that way?"

"It wasn't exactly the hand," Greg pointed out. He had followed Marisel out of the club.

"I guess I'm ready to call it a night," Lucy's father said. He carefully backed toward the parking lot. "I'll see you back at the house."

"What about Carmella?" Lucy asked.

He looked chagrined. "Dang. I almost forgot about her."

"Don't worry about her." Greg cleared his throat. "She's already found another dance partner."

He nodded. "That's good then. She's a nice girl, just a little too...energetic for me."

He began a funny sideways shuffle across the parking lot, head bent, hands to his backside. Lucy thought of him going home to their empty house—or worse, one of Gloria's crying jags—and her heart wrenched. She turned to Greg. "I'm sorry, but I can't leave him like this. I'd better go with him."

He nodded. "Yeah, I guess you'd better." He flashed a brief smile. "Call me if you need anything."

Should she tell him how many points he'd just racked up

on the boyfriend meter, or keep it a secret? She settled for a smile and a brief kiss. "Thanks," she whispered. "For everything."

He smoothed her hair back from her face. "He'll be all right, you know. He's just going through a rough patch."

"I know." A rough patch. So when did they reach smooth sailing? Or was that a myth created by the same people who told you to "walk on the sunny side of life" and other bland and useless advice?

They arrived home to an empty house, but Gloria had left a note. *At COMA Meeting. Back late. Could you pick up a few things next time you're shopping? Hummus, soy cheese, green tea, spelt flour and maybe some more SpaghettiOs?*

"So is that friend of yours moving in for good?" her father asked.

"No!" She folded the list and stuck it in the drawer under the telephone. "I'm sure she'll be moving to her own place before long." The sooner the better if their friendship was to remain intact. "I'm hoping she'll go back to her boyfriend. I'm sure they still love each other. They've just had a silly misunderstanding."

"Young people today don't want to work at staying together. Your mother and I had our problems, especially in the early days, but we didn't give up and call it quits. We kept at it."

"Because you loved each other."

"Yeah, but sometimes love is learning to ignore all the things about the other person that you don't like." He kissed the top of her head. "I'm callin' it a night, pumpkin."

"Good night, Daddy."

She was too wired to sleep, so she made a cup of tea and took it and Millie into her bedroom. She changed into pajamas, then curled up in bed with her mother's garden planner. Closing her eyes, she opened the book at random.

The pages fell open to August, and the words *Homemade solutions are often the best.* Below this was a recipe for ratatouille that had been cut from the newspaper and stuck down with tape.

Her mother made the best ratatouille! Her mouth watered at the memory. And all this time Lucy thought it was a recipe she'd created herself—a recipe lost forever now that she was gone. She smiled, remembering the fantastic dinner parties her mother loved to give. Rumor was people arranged their summer schedules and vacations around Barb Lake's parties.

Millie nuzzled against Lucy. She studied the recipe again and a warm tingling swept over her. "That's it." She hugged the dog so tightly the animal squeaked. "I'll give a dinner party. I'll invite Gloria and Dennis. Once they're together again, I'm sure they'll see how silly they're being to stay apart like this. Greg can come, too. It'll be my chance to show him that I can be conventional and domestic when I put my mind to it. Who else?"

She fished in her bedside drawer until she came up with a stub of pencil and began making a list. She needed someone to go with her father. Someone close to his own age. Someone he'd like.

She remembered Marisel admiring her father on the dance floor. Of course. Her co-worker would be perfect. She even knew about flowers, like Mom. And Mom would have liked her, she was sure.

Her tea grew cold as she made a menu and a shopping list. She wasn't much of a cook, but the ratatouille didn't look too difficult and she could fill in around it with store-bought salads and stuff. She hugged the dog close again. "I have a really good feeling about this, Millie. I just know that this time, everything's going to work out perfectly."

SHE COULD HARDLY WAIT to tell Greg about the party. As soon as he walked in the door at work the next morning she cornered him. "I've had the most marvelous idea," she said.

"Does it involve you and me, alone?" His smile could have melted butter.

"Uh, no." She laughed. "I'm going to give a dinner party."

"A dinner party? You? You've told me how many times how *un*domestic you are and now you're going to invite people over to your house and cook for them?"

"I didn't say I was completely incompetent." She raised her chin in mock offense, fighting back a smile. "I'm going to make something simple. My mother's ratatouille."

"Okay. What brought this on?"

"The idea came to me last night when I was reading Mom's gardening planner. I thought I could invite Dennis and Gloria, and they'd see how silly it was for them to be apart. And I'd invite my father and Marisel so they could get to know each other better."

"Marisel?" He looked surprised. "Why her?"

"Why not?" She leaned toward him. "She's perfect for my dad—close to his age, smart and kind. And she was admiring him on the dance floor the other night, so I definitely think she's interested."

He shook his head. "I don't know. Matchmaking sounds risky."

"It'll work out great, I just know it. And you'll come, won't you?"

"I wouldn't miss it. But a party like this is a lot of work. Are you sure you want to take all this on?"

"You don't think I can pull it off, do you? Well, you're going to be astonished at what I can do when I put my mind to it."

He chuckled. "Then I think I'd better shut up and stay out of the way. And I definitely think you're capable. I'm still counting on you to decorate my house, remember?"

"That's right. When do you want me to come over and take a look at it?"

"How about tonight? I'll even spring for dinner."

"Okay." Her dad was going to an Astros game with friends from work. Gloria had another COMA meeting. Lucy might as well go out and enjoy herself. "Tonight sounds good."

"I'll warn you, my skills in the kitchen are limited. What kind of take-out do you want—Chinese or pizza?"

"Pizza sounds good." An anticipatory tingle buzzed through her. She wasn't too worried about what they had for dinner. Dessert was what she was looking forward to.

GREG'S PLACE was about what Lucy had expected. Dark cherry furniture circa 1970, upholstered in floral velvet that had faded until the pattern looked like a washed-out watercolor, filled the living room. Tweedy brown drapes, also faded, stood out against off-white walls. A few family photos and books added the only personal touch. "So what do you think?" Greg asked.

She studied the table lamps with the bases shaped like pineapples. Exactly like the ones she'd inherited from Aunt Edna. Whoever thought these were a good idea? "It could use some updating. Fresh paint. Maybe some slipcovers. New art on the walls."

He nodded. "So what color do you think would be good in here?"

She considered the question a moment. "I think a deep plum would look great on the walls. And it would really bring out the cherry wood in this furniture."

He paled. "Purple?"

She bit her tongue to keep from laughing. "Let me guess—you were thinking beige?"

He flushed. "It's a nice, neutral color. Goes with everything."

"How many beige flowers do you use in landscapes?"

He frowned. "That's different. It's outside. And flowers are supposed to be colorful."

"So are walls. Believe me, with some bold colors and fresh fabrics, this house will be completely up-to-date and dramatic."

"I'm not a very dramatic kind of person."

She smiled. "Maybe if you lived in a dramatic house you would be."

They toured the kitchen, which thankfully did not have avocado or harvest gold appliances, but a neutral white she could work with. Then they moved on to a spare bedroom that had been turned into a home office. At least this room looked like it belonged in the twenty-first century. Greg had installed floor-to-ceiling bookshelves and a sleek-looking computer desk and artist's drawing table. A series of landscape designs were tacked to the table. She studied the drawings of bold splashes of flowers and fountains amid soaring skyscrapers. The effect was striking, like a modern art piece with flowers substituted for paint. "Is this one of your jobs?" she asked.

"It's a proposal for a job I've bid on."

He joined her at the table, standing so close she could feel the warmth of his body. She resisted the urge to lean back against him. Not yet. But soon. "Who for?"

"Allen Industries."

She turned to gape at him, not hiding her surprise. "Aren't they a huge concern?"

He nodded. "If I could land a contract with them, it would really allow me to expand the business."

She looked back at the drawings again. One showed a courtyard with a wall of water at one end, trellised roses lining the other three sides. The effect was a private retreat in the midst of a bustling business center. "These plans are beautiful. How could they turn you down?"

He shoved his hands in his pockets. "I haven't heard anything and it's been weeks since I sent this in. I figure they'll go with one of the national companies, like they always do."

"You should call them and ask for an update."

"I should. I guess I've just been afraid of finding out bad news." The corners of his mouth remained turned down.

"Don't give up already. Think positive. You'll hear good news." She turned to face him.

His gaze met hers, dark and intense, questioning. *What are you really all about? Can I trust these feelings between us?* "Are you always such an optimist?"

Are you always so cautious? But of course he was. Greg never did anything without first calculating the risks and the benefits. Could she ever live that way and not feel she was in a straight jacket? Or could she convince him to step out of his safety zone a little? She smiled. "It beats the alternative."

He shrugged. "I suppose. But at least if you prepare for the worst, you aren't setting yourself up for disappointment."

"And if you're always so cautious, aren't you missing out on some wonderful surprises?" She slipped her arms around his neck and stood on tiptoe to kiss him.

He stilled for half a second, then his arms came around her. "This is the kind of surprise I like," he murmured against her lips before deepening the kiss.

Ah, anticipation! That kiss was almost—almost—worth the long wait to be alone with him once more. Seeing him every day at the office, wondering what he was thinking, entertaining fantasies of dragging him into the storeroom and having her way with him...

He lifted his head and looked into her eyes again. This time she saw delight and lust and a surprising tenderness there. "You've been driving me crazy, do you know that?" he said, his voice gruff.

She writhed against him, impatient and deliberately provocative. "How do you think I feel, lusting after my boss when I'm supposed to be working?"

Did he actually *growl?* Could it be Mr. Conventional possessed the soul of a wild man?

Things got hot and heavy after that. The next thing she knew, she was sprawled across the desk, papers still drifting in the air around them. Greg was kissing her neck and a stapler poked her in one cheek.

"Uh, maybe we should go into the bedroom." She shifted, trying to avoid the stapler.

In answer, he scooped her into his arms and started toward the door. For the first time in her life, she thought she knew what all those books meant when they talked about women swooning in men's arms. Yowza! She could learn to like this caveman stuff.

After seeing the rest of the house, she didn't have high hopes for the bedroom, but her worst fears were not realized. At least it didn't have high school pennants on the wall and old baseball trophies on the bookshelves. The room was plain, but masculine, with a dark green comforter on the bed and blank walls.

He eased her down on the bed, then stretched out beside her. His gaze locked to hers, he stroked her face with the back of his hand. The sweet gesture brought a knot to her throat. Where was the caveman? She could handle him better. Lust she knew about. Other feelings—dare she say love?—she wasn't so sure of.

She slid one hand under his T-shirt, across the hard plain of his stomach. Her own insides quivered at the feel of his heated skin. "Why don't we get these clothes off?" she whispered. She already knew what he looked like naked from the waist up. She couldn't wait to see how magnificent the rest of him was bound to be.

He stood to undress and she sat up to do the same, avoiding looking at him as she unzipped and unbuttoned. Making love with a guy the first time was always awkward. What would he think of her naked? Would he notice the cellulite on her thighs or think her stomach was too poufy?

While the woman was obsessing over these things and trying to artfully arrange the sheets to hide her flaws, even the homeliest guy would be strutting around the bedroom with the mighty member waving in the breeze with the blues standard *I'm a man. I said a real man,* playing in his head.

Okay, so Greg didn't strut. More points in his favor. He slipped into bed and scooted over beside her. He skimmed one hand over her, stroking her as if she were some delicate flower. "What are you thinking about now?" he asked.

She blinked. Wasn't that supposed to be *her* line? "Um, I'm thinking I should have brushed my teeth before I came over here."

She'd scarcely finished the sentence when his lips covered hers in a slow, melting kiss that had her squirming against him. He lifted his head and looked at her. "You taste like oranges."

"Oh. I had a tangerine Life Saver on the way over."

"Mmmm. I like tangerines." His grin was wicked. "They're so sweet and juicy. Like you."

She was prepared with a smart-ass reply, but all she

could manage was a low moan as he slid two fingers into her. Her vision blurred and she closed her eyes and surrendered to his skillful touch.

Fantasizing about this moment, she'd imagined herself in a more active role—wowing him with her prowess, maybe even teaching him a few new tricks. But as far as she could tell, he didn't need to learn anything. He had her paralyzed with pleasure. Helpless again, but this time, she wasn't complaining.

When he moved away from her, she let out a cry of frustration and reached to pull him back. He chuckled, and she heard a foil packet tearing. "Always impatient, aren't you?"

"Are you complaining?" She looked into his eyes as he levered himself over her.

"No. I'm right there with you this time."

Then she was struck dumb again as he filled her and began to move. She might have screamed with joy. She was pretty sure her fingernails raked his back. The earth didn't move, but the bed might have, as an amazing climax rocketed through her.

Who knew? To think all these years she'd been wasting time on bad boys who turned out to be pretty tame between the sheets when she should have been going after more conventional types, who apparently saved their stuff for the bedroom.

16

Despite the gardener's best intentions, nature will improvise.

SOME TIME LATER, when Lucy had drifted back to earth and returned to her senses, she lay cuddled against Greg, a smile quite possibly permanently etched on her face. "That was fantastic," she murmured and pressed herself even closer against him.

"Yeah." He slipped his arm around her.

Okay, so he wasn't Mr. Eloquent. What man was?

"What do you want to do now?" he asked.

How about what we just did? But even wild men needed time to recover, she guessed. She trailed her hand down her chest. "Maybe I should move in with you and leave Gloria and my dad to work out their own problems." She was only half-joking.

He shifted, drawing away enough to look at her. "You're kidding, right?"

Why did he look so upset? Her own smile faltered. "Maybe. Or maybe not. What about it? Think you'd like a roommate?"

His frown was positively forbidding. "I think that would be a bad idea."

So much for her permanent smile. She sat up and stared down at him. "Why would it be such a bad idea? I mean,

I'm not saying I'd move in right away, but what if things keep going well between us? Why shouldn't we try living together?"

He sat up also. "What would people think? At work? And what about my customers?"

"What business of your customers is it? How would they even know?"

"Allen Industries does a background check on its contractors. They're notoriously conservative. I'm sure me shacking up with my office manager would go over really big."

She bristled. "Shacking up? You make it sound like I'm some tramp you picked up off the street."

"Now Lucy, you know I don't mean it like that. But come on. What would your father say?"

"My father wouldn't be living with you. And obviously, neither will I." She crawled out of bed and began searching for her clothes. It was hard to look really pissed off, much less dignified, when you were naked. She retrieved her underwear from the bedside table.

"Come on. Don't be angry. Why are we even talking about this now?"

"Why not talk about it now?" She hopped on one foot, vainly trying to insert the other foot into the leg opening of her panties. How could she possibly make her point if she fell over on top of him again? And where was her damn bra? Her breasts bounced up and down like a carnival ride. She could feel Greg's eyes on them and she was sure he was scarcely listening to her. She succeeded in fitting her leg through the opening and pulled the panties up to her waist, then snatched up her bra. "I think it's better that we find out about these differences now." She hooked the bra and looked around for her dress.

"Don't tell me you're back to that. Of course we're differ-

ent. I'm a man. You're a woman." He stood, but made no
move to find his clothes.

She spotted her dress across the room, draped over the
back of a chair. How had it ended up there? "This goes beyond that," she said. "The thing is, I enjoy challenges. Trying new things. Taking risks. You're the exact opposite.
You want everything to be a sure thing."

"That's not true. I just don't think it's a good idea to go
rushing into things without considering the consequences."

"If you don't even understand what I'm talking about,
how can we even have a rational discussion?" She pulled
the dress over her head and groped behind her for the zipper.

"No discussion with you is rational." He strode over to
her and jerked up the zipper.

"So now I'm irrational!" She found one shoe under the
bed and slipped it on, then limped around the room,
searching for the other.

"Don't twist my words." Still naked, he followed her
around the room. Apparently, arguing did something for
his libido, as parts of him showed signs of being ready for
action.

"Put some clothes on," she said, and tossed his pants to
him.

He smiled. "Maybe you should take yours off again and
we can discuss this in bed."

"I'm not going to bed with you again." She found her
other shoe and put it on, then turned to face him. "Look, I
really like you," she said. "But I don't see any point in taking this any further. We're never going to see things eye to
eye."

"What do you mean?"

"I mean I think we can never be more than just friends."

"You can say that after what just happened between us?"

Her heart skipped in her chest, remembering how she had felt, lying in his arms. She shook her head. "It was wonderful, but there's no sense getting in any deeper when we'd only end up making each other unhappy." She sighed. "Opposites may attract in books and movies, but I don't think it really works that way in real life."

He stared at her a long moment, his eyes hot with anger or passion or some other emotion she didn't want to know about. She turned away from him and he began to dress. "I'll take you back to your car," he said, walking past her and out the door.

She collected her purse in the living room and followed him out to his truck. She felt like she'd eaten worms for supper. He probably hated her now. She'd lost a lover *and* a friend and maybe even a job. Talk about screwing up her life!

The ride to her car was painfully silent. When he pulled into the nursery parking lot, she opened the door. "I understand if you don't want to come to the party next weekend," she said, not looking at him.

"I'm bringing Marisel, remember?"

"Oh, yeah." They'd decided Marisel would come with Greg, then if she and Lucy's dad seemed to be hitting it off, they'd ask her father to give Marisel a ride home.

"Besides, if I don't come, you'll have an uneven number," he said. "I'm pretty sure that's a social faux pas or something."

She nodded. "All right." Maybe he didn't totally hate her. She hazarded a glance in his direction. He was looking at her intently. "Do I still have a job?" she asked.

"Do you still want one?"

She nodded. "I meant what I said about wanting to be friends."

"Then I'll expect to see you at work in the morning." He turned the key and started the truck again. "I'm not done with you yet, Lucy Lake."

She climbed out of the truck, his words echoing in her head. She watched him drive away, wondering if it was a trick of the light, or was he really smiling?

"JUST SHOOT ME." A little over a week later, Lucy stood in the kitchen, wiping sweat from her forehead and staring at her mother's largest stockpot, which was three-quarters full of a concoction that didn't look like any ratatouille she'd ever seen. "If I ever again even suggest that a dinner party might be nice, put me out of my misery right then."

"If you'd asked me in the first place, I would have told you this was a bad idea." Gloria looked up from counting out silverware. "And I don't know why you invited Dennis. It's over between us."

"How can you say that?" She used a wooden spoon to try to mash a tomato against the inside of the pot. Maybe she should have cut them into smaller pieces. "You haven't given him a chance. I can't believe you'd give up on a relationship without making more of an effort."

"There's no point in wasting more time." Gloria snapped open a folded napkin with a flick of her wrist. "Dennis and I have completely different philosophies about life. I'm only sorry I didn't realize it before."

"Before what? Before you fell in love with him?"

Gloria's mouth quavered and her eyes grew shiny. She drew in a shaky breath and straightened her shoulders. "Love is only one component of a successful relationship. If two people don't look at life the same way, the odds of them staying together in the long run decline astronomically."

Lucy inwardly cringed. Of course she'd used the same

argument with Greg, but theirs was a special case. Anybody could see that Gloria and Dennis were so right for each other. "Says who?" she countered.

"Says the alarming divorce rate in this country, for one. Come on. Do you think your parents would have stayed together so long if they hadn't had similar opinions and goals and outlooks?"

She shrugged. "Maybe not. Or maybe they would have done even better. Maybe their differences would have added interest to their relationship. Or over time they would have come to see each other's point of view." Not that that applied to everyone. Oh, why was she even arguing the point with Gloria? She ought to be concentrating on dinner. She glanced at the clock. "Oh God. Everyone will be here in half an hour and I still need to change clothes." She turned to Gloria. "Be a peach and take those salads I bought out of the deli containers and put them in my mom's servings bowls. Please?"

"All right. What did you get?"

"A Greek salad with feta and a regular garden salad. They're from that gourmet place on the corner."

"Ooh. Expensive. Don't you know salad's the easiest thing to make?"

"It also takes time I don't have. It took me almost two hours to cut up all the vegetables for the ratatouille." She gave the stock pot one last stir and set the spoon aside and ripped off her apron. "It would have helped if the recipe was more specific. It says 'cut vegetables into chunks' but it doesn't say what size the chunks should be. And do you slice the carrots into little coins, or cut them into little sticks?"

Gloria stared at her. "Does it matter?"

"I don't know. They don't tell you these things." She

looked around the kitchen, frowning. "I keep thinking I'm forgetting something."

"Go, get dressed." Gloria made shooing motions and opened the refrigerator. "I'll take care of the salads. Everything will be fine."

Millie followed Lucy into the bedroom and jumped up on the bed. "I've been neglecting you all day, haven't I?" She patted the dog, then opened her closet door. "I've just been so worried about tonight. I want everything to be perfect."

She stripped out of her tomato-stained T-shirt and shorts and reached for the ruffled miniskirt and floral tank she'd chosen for tonight. As she dressed, she reviewed her plans for the evening. They'd have drinks and hors d'oeuvres—fancy cheeses and crackers. Then dinner with wine. The alcohol would be just enough to loosen everybody up without making them drunk. She'd seat Dennis and Gloria next to each other and put Marisel next to her father. After dinner, they'd have dessert and coffee in the living room, then she'd suggest they team up for a game of *Pictionary*. Gloria and her dad couldn't resist a competition, and working together on a project was a great way for a couple to get close. After that, she was counting on natural attraction to take care of the rest.

Of course, there'd be the whole awkwardness with Greg to get through, but they'd been managing all right at work this past week, mainly by avoiding each other or by being painfully polite when they did have to interact. Greg was especially aggravating, because he acted like nothing at all had happened between them, when all she had to do was look at him and her body reacted with the memory of his hands and lips on her. While her mind was trying to be mature and plan for her future, her hormones were perpetual teenagers, urging her to forget about tomorrow and enjoy herself today.

Hormones apparently didn't know much about broken hearts, but she'd had hers cracked enough times to want to avoid the possibility altogether. Especially since, the way Greg made her feel, he might be the one to do permanent damage.

Marisel had given them a few questioning looks, but she'd wisely said nothing, keeping the conversation to work topics and discussion of tonight's party.

Lucy had never realized how much work went into a simple dinner. She'd spent the past week cleaning, shopping and preparing. She'd hauled out her mother's best china and linens, ordered flowers, polished silver and even set out the fancy guest soaps and towels that no one ever used. Every time she thought she was through, she'd remember something else her mother had done to make her parties perfect. And she definitely wanted tonight to be perfect.

The doorbell rang as she was putting the finishing touches on her lipstick. She slipped into high-heeled sandals and raced to the door, pausing a few steps away to collect herself. She checked the peep hole and saw Dennis waiting on the front stoop, a bunch of flowers in his hand.

"Hello, Dennis. How are you this evening?" She thought it was a good sign that he'd arrived first. He must be eager to see Gloria again.

"Hey, Luce." He thrust the flowers toward her. "These are for you."

"How sweet." She ushered him into the living room, where Gloria was fiddling with the stereo. "Gloria, look at the lovely flowers Dennis brought."

"Dennis brought flowers?" Gloria raised her eyebrows.

"Hey, I can be a gentleman when I want to." He walked over to stand beside her. "How are you doing?"

"I'm fine." She was playing it cool, pretending indifference, but her cheeks were flushed, her eyes bright.

The doorbell rang again and she let in Greg and Marisel. The older woman greeted her with a kiss on the cheek. "I am so happy to be in your home," she said. "Thank you for inviting me."

"I'm so glad you could come." She returned the kiss, then looked up and found herself caught by Greg's gaze.

"Hello, Lucy. You look beautiful tonight, as always."

In spite of her vow to play it cool around him, she blushed. "Thank you. You look very nice yourself." He wore slacks and a pale green shirt and he smelled of some spicy cologne. She felt dizzy standing this close to him, then realized she'd been holding her breath. She let it out and fixed what she hoped was a pleasant smile on her face. "Won't you come in."

By this time her father had made it into the living room. She led Marisel over to him. "Daddy, this is Marisel Luna, one of the horticulturists at the nursery where I work. Marisel, this is my father, Frank Lake. He's an electrician."

Her father's smile was positively dazzling. "Nice to meet you Marisel. That's a beautiful name. Very lyrical."

Marisel positively beamed. "It was my mother's name."

"Is that so? Are you from Mexico?"

"I'm originally from Guatemala, though I've lived in the United States for many years now."

"Guatemala? Is that in South America?"

"Central America. Near..."

With things well in hand here, Lucy checked Dennis and Gloria. They were standing by the patio doors, deep in conversation. She picked up a tray of cheese and crackers and carried it over to them. "Would you like an hors d'oeuvre?" she asked.

Gloria selected several chunks of cheese from the tray. "I was just telling Dennis about COMA's campaign against Allen Industries," she said. "There's a rally at their head-quarters this evening."

Lucy glanced nervously toward Greg, but he was over by the bar, opening the wine. The last thing she wanted was for him to find out about Gloria's animosity toward his coveted client.

"Who has a protest on a Saturday evening?" Dennis asked. "Nobody will be at work then."

"We don't have to compete with anyone else for news coverage then," Gloria said. "And if we're lucky, we'll make the front page of the Sunday paper. It's all part of our strategy."

"I can't believe you waste so much energy on a lost cause like that and you can't find the time to come to one lousy show of mine." He popped a cracker into his mouth and chewed furiously.

"I'm doing something important to make this world a better place." She glared at him.

"And you don't think making people laugh makes the world a better place? Let me tell you, there are people out there who really need a laugh when they come to hear me. I could be saving lives for all you know."

Gloria rolled her eyes. "Honestly, I—"

"Why don't we all go into dinner now?" Lucy interrupted, before Gloria got too wound up. Maybe when they sat down to eat, these two would be in a better mood. She was still sure they had a chance, if they'd only listen to their hearts instead of spouting their opinions on things that had nothing to do with how they felt about each other.

She brought the ratatouille from the kitchen and joined

everyone else in the dining room. Greg pulled out her chair for her. "Relax," he whispered in her ear. "Everything's going to be fine."

She gave him a grateful smile. Maybe she couldn't be anything more than friends with Greg, but that was something, wasn't it? If only she had his confidence that tonight would be a success.

She passed her mother's soup tureen to Greg and he ladled up a large serving of ratatouille and passed the tureen to Gloria. Gloria served her own helping and wrinkled her nose at the concoction in her dish.

Lucy swallowed hard. She had to admit the ratatouille looked odd. Sort of grayish. And lumpy. Her father poked at his serving with a spoon. "What is this supposed to be?" he asked.

"It's ratatouille." She unfolded her napkin in her lap and attempted a smile. "It's Mother's recipe."

Her father looked doubtful. "I don't remember your mother ever making anything that looked like this."

"I'm sure it's delicious." Greg spooned up a large bite and ate it with gusto. The effect was spoiled, however, when he immediately spit out something and examined it. "Uh, I think you're supposed to take the labels off the tomatoes before you cook them."

She flushed. "I must have missed one." She took a tentative taste. It wasn't bad. But the texture wasn't great. Sort of mushy.

"I think you cooked it too long," her father said.

"No. It's very good this way. Easier to digest." Marisel gave her an encouraging smile.

"You have problems with your digestion?" her father asked.

Marisel frowned at him. "No. And what kind of question is that to ask a person?"

"You're the one who brought it up."

"The salad is really good." Dennis came to her rescue this time.

"The salad is from the deli," Gloria said. "That national chain down the street." She leaned toward Lucy. "You should have gone to Armando's across town. Then you'd be supporting a local business."

"What about the gas she'd waste driving across town?" Dennis asked. "Wouldn't that be polluting the environment?"

"Since when do you care about pollution?" Gloria asked.

"Hey, I'm not some insensitive oaf, you know. I'm the one who installed all those fluorescent bulbs to save energy, then you made me take them out."

"Fluorescent lighting gives me headaches."

"Life is full of compromises, Gloria. Why can't you realize that?"

"Dennis, would you pass me the salad?" Greg made an attempt to waylay the argument.

"But it's usually the woman who compromises, isn't it?" Marisel inserted herself into the conversation.

"You women have it made," her father countered. "You should try being a man these days. We never know how we're supposed to act."

"How can you say that?" Marisel countered. "Women—"

"Lucy, the table really looks beautiful," Greg tried again. But everyone ignored him, including Lucy, who watched in horror as the meal she'd slaved over went practically untouched while everyone argued over whether men or women had it tougher. The party that was supposed to bring everyone together had turned into a battle of the sexes!

"Would anyone like dessert?" she asked, raising her voice to be heard above the quarrel.

For a moment, she thought she'd succeeded in diverting their attention. "What are we having?" Gloria asked.

"Crème brulée."

"Did you make it?" her father asked.

"Uh...yes." The filling had only curdled slightly, though she'd successfully disguised this with a liberal application of whipped cream.

"I think I'll pass." Her father pushed his plate away. "I appreciate the effort, hon, but maybe next time you should order out."

"What a mean thing to say to your own daughter," Marisel raised her voice in Lucy's defense.

"I only call 'em like I see 'em. You tell me that meal wasn't awful."

"The salad was good," Dennis said again.

"Spoken by a man who thinks ramen noodles are gourmet cuisine," Gloria said.

"If you were home nights to eat dinner with me I might go to more trouble," he said. "As it is, you're always off to some rally or protest or consciousness raising meeting."

"If you'd come with me sometimes, you might learn something!"

Lucy pushed her own plate away and stood. No one even noticed. Even Greg was caught up in the argument between her father and Marisel. Fighting tears, she turned and fled.

17

Your greatest discoveries in the garden often come by accident.

LUCY RETREATED to the back patio, a place she hadn't been in weeks, because it depressed her too much to look at her mother's dead roses. Yet another in her list of failures. She couldn't even host a simple dinner party without it turning into a fiasco.

"Mom's probably beside herself if she can see me right now," she said to Millie as the little dog joined her outside.

Millie's whimper sounded sympathetic, but with a dog you couldn't really tell, could you? "I wanted so much for everyone to be happy," she said, staring into the darkness. "Mom would have made it all work out. She always knew what to do."

She thought of all the advice in her mother's garden planner. The book had been a surprising help to her these past few weeks. Still, there probably wasn't anything in there to address this evening's disaster.

Who was she kidding? Her whole *life* was a disaster. She'd even managed to fall in love with a man who was so different from her they were doomed to failure. Despite all her lectures about integrity and not overlooking decent, honest men without a lot of flash, even Mom would have realized that someone as conservative as Greg and someone as flighty as Lucy would sooner or later drive each other away.

"You should have seen his face when I suggested we move in together," she told Millie. "He was positively appalled. And not from a moral standpoint either. That I could understand. No, he was worried about what people would think. What a *corporation* would think." Her shoulders slumped. "Some stranger's opinion was more important to him than our happiness."

Millie whimpered again, and nudged Lucy's leg with her nose. Lucy leaned down to pet her. "At least you're not ashamed to hang out with a screwup like me. I guess dogs aren't particular that way."

To her shock, Millie bit down on her bracelet, narrowly missing her wrist. She gasped and tried to pull away, but the dog held tight. "Let go!" she cried. "What do you think you're doing?"

But the dog ignored her, holding fast to the bracelet and tugging Lucy away from the patio, out into the yard. Lucy stumbled along after her, fumbling for the catch of the bracelet, unable to find it in her panic. A person had sunk to a new low when her own dog tried to bite her.

She was ready to scream for help when Millie stopped, though the dog kept a firm hold on the bracelet. "Let go!" Lucy cried, trying to shake free.

The dog looked away from her and wagged its tail. Lucy stopped and watched her. "What are you looking at?"

She followed the dog's gaze and gasped at what she saw. In the pale glow of a streetlamp shining over the back fence, a single blossom shone, surrounded by glossy green leaves.

She took off running, dragging the dog with her now. Millie released her hold on the bracelet and Lucy skidded to a stop in front of the Queen Elizabeth rosebush. She stared, heart pounding, at the sight before her, and let out a soft sigh.

The pride of her mother's garden had been pruned to a shadow of its former glory. The last time Lucy had noticed it, it had been a scraggly cane with only a few yellowing leaves. But by some miracle the bush was now transformed, covered with dozens of fist-sized pink roses.

GREG SAW LUCY run from the table and started to follow her, but Marisel put out a restraining hand. "Let her go," the older woman advised. "She's upset and needs to be alone."

"I don't know why she's upset," her father said. "All I said was that next time she should order out. Everybody knows she can't cook worth a darn. It's never been a big deal before."

"Maybe she wanted to impress someone," Marisel said, giving Greg a significant look.

He flushed. "I never asked her to cook for me," he said. "I don't give a damn if she can boil water. She doesn't have to do anything for me but keep on being Lucy."

"Have you told her that?" Marisel asked.

He looked away. "She won't listen to me."

"Then maybe you should show her how you feel instead of talking."

He stared at the older woman. Wasn't that what he'd been doing all this time? He'd asked her to help him at his house because he wanted to show her he valued her opinion. He told her all the time how beautiful she was. He encouraged all her ideas, even this crazy dinner party. What else was he supposed to do to show her how much he cared for her? How much he loved her?

The thought made him light-headed. Yes, he was in love with the most aggravating, contrary, stubborn woman on the face of this earth. And there wasn't a damn bit of good it was going to do him as long as she thought he was some stick-in-the-mud geek who would cross the street to avoid anything new and different.

So maybe there was a little truth in that. That didn't mean he wanted to change *her*. He figured she was daring enough for both of them. Besides, couldn't he learn to love more risk, if it meant having her love him, too?

He swallowed a sudden lump in his throat. He didn't see how he would ever convince her of that.

"We're leaving now." He looked up, surprised to see Dennis and Gloria standing by his chair. "Where's Lucy?"

"Uh, she had to step out for a minute."

"Tell her goodbye for us, okay?"

"And thanks for the dinner," Dennis said.

"So...you're leaving together?" Five minutes ago, they'd been at each other's throats.

Gloria glanced at Dennis. "I told Den he couldn't criticize me if he didn't know anything about the work I do, so he said he'd come with me to the protest tonight."

Dennis took her hand. "And she agreed to come to my next *Laugh Stop* gig."

"This still doesn't mean I'm moving back in with you," she said.

"We'll take it one day at a time, okay?"

They left and Marisel stood and began gathering up plates. "We shouldn't leave all these dirty dishes for Lucy to do."

"Let me help you with that." Lucy's father took the stack of plates from Marisel. "This old china is heavy."

"It's a beautiful pattern," she said.

"My late wife picked it out for our wedding." He nodded toward the kitchen. "Come on. I'll show you where the dishwasher is."

"Are you crazy? You have to handwash china like this."

They left Greg alone. He stared at the remains of the meal and thought of Lucy out there in the yard. Was she crying? Would she be angry with him if he went to her now?

He knew only one way to find out. He shoved out of his chair and headed for the patio doors.

He found her kneeling at the other end of the yard. His heart stopped beating, and he wondered if she was hurt. Had she tripped or fallen? Suddenly taken ill? He ran to her, stopping a few feet away to stare at the roses.

It would be years before the Queen Elizabeth returned to its former glory, but the stunted bush that was left had made a good show. The big pink blossoms filled this corner of the garden with their sweet perfume.

Lucy sat with a blossom in her lap. She stroked the pink petals and smiled. Millie watched, too, a look like wonder on the funny dog's face.

Millie was the first to see him. She looked up and whimpered, wagging her pom-pom tail. Lucy looked up then, her smile still in place. "Isn't it wonderful?" she breathed.

He knelt beside her and touched the velvet petals. "It's beautiful." *Like you.* But he didn't say it. She hadn't paid much attention to his words before and nothing had happened to change that.

She looked back at the bloom in her lap. "I can't believe I did it. *You* did it. You saved Mom's roses."

"You deserve some credit, too. If you hadn't called me when you did, they wouldn't have made it." He looked at the bloom-laden bush. "Your mom would be proud."

"At least I did one thing right." She hung her head. "The dinner party was a bust."

He glanced back toward the house. He could just make out Marisel and Lucy's father, side by side at the kitchen sink. "Oh, I don't know about that."

"This was supposed to bring everyone together. Instead, they're all fighting."

He reached out and took her hand. She didn't immediately pull away, so he took that as a good sign. "Gloria and Dennis left together to go to some protest meeting. And your dad and Marisel are doing the dishes. They're probably bickering about the correct way to do them, but I think they both secretly enjoy the sparring."

She glanced toward the kitchen window and smiled. "I don't believe it."

"Believe it. They're all together. For now, anyway. So you deserve congratulations." He leaned forward and kissed her, lightly, on the lips. He wanted more, but how much more was up to her.

She looked at him, eyes wide. "You're a very special man, Greg. I wish we were more alike."

"We're more alike than you think." He traced the curve of her cheek with one finger. Her skin was as soft as the rose petals.

She shook her head and stood. "I'd better go in now, before we both do something we'll regret later."

He wanted to argue with her about that, but she turned and called the dog. "Millie! Time to go in now."

But the dog was nowhere to be seen. "Maybe someone let her back inside already," he said.

She shrugged. "Maybe so."

He followed her inside. In the kitchen, her father was drying while Marisel washed. "Have you seen Millie?" Lucy asked.

Her father shook his head. "She hasn't been in here."

"She's usually right under our feet," Lucy said. "She hates to miss out on anything." She went to the yard and called again, then returned to the kitchen. "She's gone."

"Maybe she's in one of the bedrooms," Greg said.

"No, the doors are all closed. And I checked the living room and dining room. Besides, if she was here, she'd be with us." She hugged her arms across her chest. "She must have gotten out of the fence. We've got to find her before she gets hurt."

"Come on. We'll look right away." He put his hand on her shoulder and steered her to the door. "Don't worry. We'll find her. Everything will be all right."

"That's what you always say."

"And I believe it."

"You haven't had my life."

"Stick with me and you might change your luck."

She shook her head, but her eyes held a light that gave him hope. Maybe if he found her dog, he'd be the hero he wanted to be in her eyes. Or at least she'd see that sometimes two mismatched halves could make a more interesting whole.

WHY WAS LIFE *lately one screwup after another?* Lucy thought as she and Greg walked the street in front of her house, calling for Millie. Just when things seemed to be evening out for her, something awful happened. There was no sign of the poodle. It was as if she'd vanished into thin air. "Maybe we'd better drive around and look," she said. Her hands shook as she dug in her purse for her car keys. *Oh God, please don't let anything happen to Millie.* In a short time, she'd become so attached to that goofy little dog.

What if she'd gotten into traffic and been hit by a car? What if she was lost?

What if she'd gone back to wherever she came from originally? There'd be some small comfort in knowing she was okay, but how could she bear to give her up?

Greg rested a hand on her shoulder. "I'll drive. You can

watch for her. If we don't see her while we're driving around, we'll come back here and go door to door."

He was so calm. So organized. She gave him a grateful look. "Thanks. That's a good plan." Always before she'd put down logic and order as dull and predictable, but there was something to be said for that kind of solid dependability at a time like this.

She handed him her keys and followed him to her car. Her stomach was still in knots, but she felt a little calmer, knowing she wasn't trying to find Millie by herself. Trouble was easier to handle if you didn't have to deal with it alone.

They headed out, not saying anything. She pressed her forehead against the window, searching the passing scenery for some sign of a scruffy apricot poodle. "I hope someone didn't pick her up, thinking she was a stray," she said. "I've been meaning to take her and have her groomed, but I haven't had time." She berated herself for not making the time.

"We'll find her," Greg said. "We won't stop looking until we do."

She wanted to believe him. But nothing else in her life had turned out the way she wanted lately.

"Did you ever have a dog?" she asked when the silence in the car became unbearable.

"We always had a dog when I was growing up. I had a beagle named Bailey once who was the smartest dog. He'd always walk up to the end of our driveway to meet the bus when I got home from school. And when I was in high school my dad got a blue heeler he named Andy. That dog would go crazy, playing in the sprinklers."

He smiled, and despite her worry over Millie, she found herself smiling too. "You should get another dog."

He nodded. "I've been thinking a lot about it lately. It would be nice to come home to a pet in the evening, you know? But then, it wouldn't be fair to the dog to leave it alone all day while I'm working."

"The work you do, you could take a dog with you. Look at Millie. She loves gardening."

"Not every dog is like Millie, but you have a point. I could probably train a dog and take it with me."

Her cell phone rang and she grabbed it up, heart pounding. "Lucy. Where are you?" Gloria's voice sounded urgent.

"Right down the street from my house. Why?" She didn't have time to go into this with Gloria.

"There's a dog here who looks exactly like Millie."

"Oh my gosh!" Hope rose up in her chest like a big balloon. "Where are you?"

"At Allen Industries headquarters. Remember, I told you COMA is having a rally here tonight?"

She looked at Greg. "Gloria says she thinks she's spotted Millie."

"Where?"

"At Allen Industries headquarters." She spoke into the phone again. "What's Millie doing?"

"She's mingling with some of the protesters."

"Okay. Don't let her out of your sight. We'll be right there."

She ended the call and sagged back against the seat.

"What's Gloria doing at Allen Industries?" Greg asked.

"She's part of a protest group. I think they're trying to convince the company to stop using chemicals or producing chemicals or something."

He frowned. "They're crazy."

"It *is* Gloria." She stared out the window. "How did a little dog like Millie end up all the way downtown?"

Greg signaled to change lanes. "Maybe she got into Gloria's car when no one was looking."

"But she was outside with me when Gloria and Dennis left."

"I don't know then, but Millie's not exactly an ordinary dog."

The scene in front of Allen Industries headquarters looked more like a block party than a protest. There were colorful costumes, including one woman who was dressed as a giant preying mantis. Two men with bongos provided percussion for a group of people with signs who had formed a conga line. The signs read *Organic—It's a Natural Thing!* and *Stop Poisoning Us!* Portable floodlights spotlighted the steps leading to the main entrance, where someone had set up a mike and a bearded man in a stocking cap was leading the crowd in a chant of "No more chemicals! No more chemicals!" The protesters chanted along more or less in rhythm, including Gloria. Dennis stood beside her, looking amused.

Closer to the street, a crowd had gathered. Most of the people looked as if they'd just come from the restaurants or theaters in the vicinity, though there were a few street people, and a group of men and women with notepads, cameras and recorders who had to be the press. And there were a few police officers, standing on alert to keep order.

Greg slid the car in behind a Channel Two news van and they hurried up to Gloria. "Where's Millie?" Lucy asked as soon as she was within speaking distance.

Gloria squinted into the crowd. "I don't know. I was trying to keep an eye on her, but I had so much else to worry about." She rung her hands. "And we've got more trouble now."

"What's wrong?" Greg asked. He had to raise his voice to be heard over a sudden fanfare from the drummers.

Gloria glanced toward center stage. "It's almost time for me to make my speech."

"Wait a minute," Lucy grabbed her arm. "What's this 'big trouble'?"

"Someone called Allen Industries execs and they came rushing out here. Which is great, because that will give us a chance to state our case to them face-to-face. But of course they weren't in a good mood and instead of listening to us, they've been doing everything they can think of to hassle us."

"Gloria, we don't really have time for this." Lucy hopped from one foot to the other in impatience.

"Wait, I'm getting to my point. Anyway, besides cutting off the electricity to the plug where we'd attached our lights and sound, they called the police. But we have a permit and everything, so there's nothing they can do. Then someone saw Millie and called the dogcatcher. He's on his way over here right now."

Lucy's stomach sank to somewhere around her ankles. It was

bad enough that Millie had run away, but she couldn't bear the thought of her in jail. She turned to Greg. "We've got to find Millie before the dogcatcher does. We just have to."

18

Just when you think you know everything about gardening, you're sure to find out you don't.

OF ALL THE PLACES Greg didn't want to be right now, this was it. If any of Allen Industries bigwigs saw him, he could kiss that contract goodbye forever.

But he couldn't turn his back on Lucy. His only hope was to find Millie and get out of there before anyone spotted him.

"Why don't you take that side of the grounds and I'll take the other and we'll see if we can find her," he suggested.

Lucy agreed and they split up. He started working his way through the crowd, alternately calling Millie's name and searching among the protesters. He didn't see the little dog, but he narrowly avoided running into the Facilities Manager, Davidson. The Allen Industries executive was arguing with a woman in pigtails about the placement of the generator the group was using to power their lights and sound system. "This is a public sidewalk and we have a permit to be here," the woman screamed shrilly.

"I don't care what that permit says, you are creating a public nuisance and libeling the name of a reputable company. If you people do not cease and desist this minute we will file suit to recover damages."

"Then we'll file suit to recover the damages you've exacted on the environment all these years," the woman countered.

Greg melted back into the shadows and bumped into Lucy. "Any luck?" she asked.

He shook his head and glanced back toward the woman and the generator. Davidson was no longer there. He turned to Lucy again. "Why are Gloria and her friends doing this?"

"Apparently, they're asking companies like Allen Industries to eliminate the use of chemicals and pesticides at their plants. And they want them to develop organic alternatives to their products."

"That's ludicrous," he said.

"I agree, but I think their hope is if they make a long list of outrageous demands, they'll end up with a few more modest concessions."

"Such as?"

"I don't know. Hormone-free beef in the company cafeteria? Organic fertilizer on the flowers and grass on the grounds?"

He frowned. "I already use organic products. They're cheaper and just as effective, besides not being poisonous to humans."

"There you go. You can agree some of their points have merit."

He looked at the circus around him and shook his head. "This isn't the way to do it."

"I think you're right, but I don't care about that now. I just want to find Millie."

Gloria was on the makeshift stage now, making an impassioned speech. Greg caught something about "civic duty" and "responsibility to the future." Dennis stood to one side, taking notes. "What's he doing?" Greg asked.

Lucy stood on tiptoe and squinted toward the stage. "I have no idea. I was the under the impression he thought all this was ridiculous."

Greg was about to say that he agreed with Dennis when a uniformed officer carrying a long pole with a noose on the end passed in front of the stage. "It's the dogcatcher!" Lucy grabbed his arm. "And look, there's Millie!"

The dog was less than ten feet from her pursuer, investigating a hot dog wrapper someone had dropped. The dogcatcher apparently hadn't seen her yet, but it wouldn't be long before he did.

"I'll distract him while you get Millie." Not waiting for his answer, she made a beeline for the dogcatcher.

He shrugged and headed toward the stage. Almost immediately, he collided with Davidson.

"Polhemus! What are you doing here?"

Greg's heart jumped up into his throat. "I...I was at dinner with my girlfriend when we saw the commotion and stopped to see what was going on." It wasn't a complete lie, after all. He made an effort to look much calmer than he felt. "Is there anything I can do to help, sir?"

Davidson looked around them. "You can explain why these nut cases feel the need to disrupt a legitimate business with their insane demands. By Lucifer!" He swore as a camera crew and reporter set up in front of the stage. "We'll be running damage control for weeks on this. I'd better go speak to that reporter." He began pushing his way toward the stage.

Greg felt as if all the air had been punched out of him as he stared after Davidson. Maybe he'd been so distracted by everything else his encounter with Greg wouldn't really register. At least maybe he'd bought the story about Greg just passing by and wouldn't hold his presence here against him.

He looked for Lucy and was surprised to see her talking with the dogcatcher. Judging by the scowl on the man's face, things weren't going so well. Had he already captured Millie?

But then he spotted the dog. Unfortunately, she was on stage with Gloria. Not exactly inconspicuous. Maybe Gloria would grab her and that will be the end of that.

But Gloria was too caught up in her speech to even notice the dog. "Instead of being one of the leading polluters in our state, COMA is calling on Allen Industries to lead the way in instituting green business practices. Recycling in all their facilities. Tough antipollution measures. Organic soap in the company restrooms!"

Maybe he could signal her…. He raised his arms and waved, hoping the news cameras wouldn't decide to pan the crowd just then.

But the only one who noticed him was Millie. The dog barked and wagged her tail, and he would have sworn she looked right at him. People turned around to see what had attracted the dog's attention.

Davidson, who'd been talking to one of the reporters near the stage, turned also. Greg ducked his head.

When he glanced up again, Davidson was talking to the reporter again, but Millie continued to stare at him.

Another reporter said something to Davidson and he turned around, saw Millie and started gesturing toward her. His face was almost purple with rage.

Does he know how ridiculous he looks? Greg wondered. And on camera, too. He wasn't exactly helping Allen Industries' cause with his outburst.

When he thought about it, a lot of things about Allen Industries had an air of the absurd. All their questions about morality. Their insistence that everyone think like they did. His father hadn't raised him to be that way.

Maybe the real reason his father had never gotten an Allen Industries' contract was that he'd refused to adhere to all their silly dictates.

Lucy was still talking to the dogcatcher. Meanwhile, Davidson had left the reporter and was advancing on Millie. The man's face was red, veins pounding at the temples. And a news camera was catching the whole sorry scene on tape.

Millie barked and wagged her tail at Greg again. Her intelligent brown eyes met his. She seemed to be sending him a message. *You know the right thing to do.* He rubbed his eyes. He must have had too much wine with dinner if he thought a dog was trying to communicate with him.

He looked at Lucy. She'd caught sight of Millie now, but a policeman had joined the argument with the dogcatcher and had her by the arm.

"Polhemus!" Davidson's shout cut through the crowd noise. He motioned toward Greg. "Don't just stand there. Help me catch that dog."

"I CAN'T BELIEVE my luck, running into you here today." Lucy inserted herself between the dogcatcher and the stage and gave him an openly flirtatious smile. She would pretend interest in a toothless humpback if it meant saving Millie. The dogcatcher's name badge identified him as Simmons. She tried for a sultry tone. "Tell me, Officer Simmons, are you here because you're interested in saving the environment?"

"Excuse me, Miss, but I'm working."

He tried to move around him, but she stepped into his path. "You are? Really? It must be fate!"

She didn't blame him for looking confused. Frankly, she wasn't sure what was going to come out of her mouth next. Anything to stall him. "I've been thinking of calling the dogcatcher. Or is animal control the preferred term these days? Of course, you can never really control animals, can you? They can be so contrary." Maybe the words weren't inspired or even very coherent, but there were a lot of them, and every one of them bought time for Millie to get away.

"Miss, I really need to get by." Simmons looked annoyed.

"But I haven't told you my problem yet." She stood her ground, refusing to let him pass. What was her problem? Besides this stubborn man and her runaway dog and her confused relationship with Greg and her worries about her father and... She considered unloading all this on the hapless dogcatcher, but decided on a completely made up— and probably more believable—story.

"You see, it's my neighbors. They have this dog. A *huge* dog. A Newfoundland or a Rottweiler or, what do they call them? Great Dane? That's it. A Great Dane. And it barks. Enormous barks. They shake the windows." She spread her hands wide, as if demonstrating the size of this imaginary dog and its prodigious barks.

Simmons was buying none of it. So much for her future on the stage. She rushed on, her voice pleading. "It's the most *horrible* sound. It wakes me up every morning. You can't imagine how terrible it is to try to work every day when you haven't slept the night before. I'm afraid I'll lose my job. If I do, do you think I can sue the neighbors?"

"Ma'am, I wouldn't know. Why don't you call the office about that? Now, if you'll excuse me..."

"No." She clutched his arm. "Don't leave me, please."

Okay, so he thought she was nuts. Maybe she was. But she couldn't let him capture Millie.

"Is there some trouble here?"

Uh-oh. She looked over her shoulder and into the eyes of a police officer. She gave a weak smile. "Trouble?"

He looked at her hand on the dogcatcher's sleeve. "What's going on here?"

"This woman is interfering with my pursuit of a stray." Simmons glared at her.

She straightened and pressed one hand to her chest in exaggerated affront. "Is that what you were doing? I had no *idea*. I was just trying to tell you about my problem."

The officer nodded. "Okay, Simmons. Looks like just a little misunder—"

"But I can't believe you'd go after a defenseless little dog." Lucy stepped in front of the dogcatcher once more as he tried to make a break for the stage. "I mean, honestly, don't you have better things to do? Aren't there rabid dogs that need to be locked up or something?"

"Miss!" Simmons glared at her and shoved past. The police officer reached out to grab her, but she ducked free and ran after the dogcatcher.

She caught up with him at the stage, where Greg and an Allen Industries' executive had also gathered.

"Finally!" The executive greeted the dogcatcher. "There's the mutt." He pointed to where Millie sat on stage, just out of reach. He turned to Greg. "If the three of us surround it, we can nab it."

Greg folded his arms across his chest. "What do you intend to do with her?"

The executive frowned at Greg. "I'm going to turn her over to the dogcatcher. And when I find out whose dog it is, I'll have the owner arrested."

Lucy gasped, but the two men paid no attention to her. They were both focused on Greg, who looked back at them with withering disdain. "Arrested? It's just a little dog. She's not hurting anything."

"What did you say?" The executive drew himself up

to his full height, which was a good six inches shorter than Greg.

"It's just a little dog. You're not helping Allen Industries' reputation with the public by going after her."

"And what would you know about our reputation?"

"I know that chasing down cute little dogs isn't a good way to enhance it."

"As if anyone pays attention to anything having to do with rabble like this." The man looked around them and shook his head.

"But you don't think the sight of you manhandling a little poodle will make them interested?"

"You two can debate this all day, but I'm going after the dog." Simmons took the steps to the top of the stage two at a time.

"No!" Lucy raced after him, followed by Greg and the man from Allen Industries. Gloria even stopped her speech and turned to stare at them.

Millie saw them coming and ducked behind a box of printed flyers, then wound around, between Gloria's legs, over a tangle of sound system cables, headed for the crowd again. "Somebody stop her!" Lucy cried. If Millie got into the crowd—or heaven forbid, the street—they might never see her again.

Simmons's catch loop reached toward the poodle, but she darted away. The Allen Industries' exec made a grab for her, tripped on the cables and went sprawling, a news station's microphone capturing every curse he shouted. Later, the public would be treated to the film, edited to a series of obnoxious bleeps.

The police officer had gotten into the act now, attempting to restore order to the crowd that surged forward. Lucy lost track of Millie as more people climbed onto the makeshift stage. "Somebody do something!" she shouted.

At that moment, she caught sight of Greg on the bottom step. Simmons was right beside him, catch loop ready. They both dove at the same time and the crowd surged around them.

Lucy closed her eyes, imagining the men trampled to death. To think her last memory of Greg would be of him so gallantly defending her—or at least her dog—before a television audience and a man who probably had the power to deny him the big contract he'd wanted most. How could she have ever accused him of valuing others' opinions too much? He'd put everything on the line for her today.

And now she might never have a chance to tell him how much that meant to her.

"Lucy, open your eyes."

She opened them, and saw Greg walking toward her, a wriggling Millie in his arms.

He didn't have a chance to get any closer. She ran into his arms, and before he could say a word, she was kissing him. An earth-shattering, heart pounding, damn-I-love-you kiss to end all kisses.

When they finally came up for air, the crowd was cheering, and the police office was tapping her on the shoulder. Dazed, she blinked at him. "Yes?"

"Ma'am, is that your dog?" He nodded to Millie, who sat in Greg's arms as regal as a princess.

"Uh, yes, it is." She mustered a shaky smile. "And I know she shouldn't be loose, but you see, she ran away, and I was absolutely frantic, and as you can see now, she's perfectly harmless and I won't let it happen again and…"

"How much is the fine?" Greg interrupted them, reaching for his wallet.

"That depends on the judge." He took out a ticket book and wrote out a citation. "Call the number on here and they'll tell you when to appear in court," he said, and handed the ticket to Lucy.

"Oh. Okay." She stared at the ticket. All things considered, she guessed she'd gotten off lightly.

The officer left and she glanced around at the crowd, which was already breaking up. She spotted Gloria and Dennis by the steps, helping to pack up the sound equipment. "I guess we'd better go," Greg said. "And lock up our little escapee here."

She nodded and fell into step beside him toward her car. "Who was that man you were talking to?"

"That was the Facilities Manager for Allen Industries."

His expression was calm, with no hint of disappointment. Still he had to be a *little* upset, right? "I guess this means you won't win the contract now."

"No, I don't imagine I will."

"You risked losing that contract to save Millie."

He nodded. "I've been doing a lot of thinking this past week. About what's really important." He looked at her and their eyes met. "You're right. I have been living too cautiously."

She ducked her head. "I've been thinking, too. Maybe I don't have to always be so impetuous." She shrugged. "Being more conventional doesn't mean I have to compete with my mom for homemaker of the year."

He slipped his arm around her. "Your mom always loved you just the way you were."

"I realize that now." She glanced over her shoulder, and saw Davidson climbing the steps to the front door of Allen Industries. "I'm still sorry this happened. I know how much you wanted that job."

He shrugged. "I thought I wanted it, but you know what?"

"What?"

His smile made her feel light enough to levitate. "I want you more." He kissed her again, a powerful, intense silent communication of all the feelings that zinged between them that neither one of them had been brave enough to acknowledge before now.

When he finally raised his head, she blinked at him, her eyes slightly glazed. "Wow!"

"Lucy, will you move in with me now? You can teach me how to be a wild man."

She laughed. "I don't have to teach you anything."

He put his arm around her shoulders and they began walking back to the car. "Does that mean you'll move in with me?"

Her stomach shimmied. Not at the thought of moving in with Greg, but at the other idea that came to her. "I think we should date first. And see where that leads."

"Are you being cautious?"

She smiled. "Let's just say I might be ready for a more traditional approach to romance." An approach her mother would no doubt applaud. *See, Mom, I've been paying attention. It just took me a while to see that you were right all along. You didn't think I'd ever admit that, did you?*

"I realized something tonight, in the garden," she said.

He stopped and turned to face her. "What did you realize?"

"That, in a way, my mother is still with me, still looking out for me and giving me advice. If what she had to say in her garden planner helped me so much, it could help other people, too."

"And?"

She hugged him, scarcely able to contain the excitement that fizzed through her. "I've decided I'm going to write a book. With all of mother's advice. I'll call it *Wisdom From the Garden.*"

He looked thoughtful "I like it. Do you think it will sell?"

"Why not? Self-help books are popular. And this one will really help people." She brushed his hair back from his forehead. "So you see, I can't move in with your right now. I'm going to be too busy with my new career."

The look in his eyes warmed her down to her toes. If he believed in her this much—and if she believed in herself—maybe her life wasn't so screwed up after all.

"I love you, did you know that?" he said.

She nodded. "I love you, too. Isn't it amazing?"

"You're amazing, Lucy Lake. Truly amazing."

"Then we make a great pair." She leaned her head on his shoulder and put her arms around him. "I think Mom would approve."

"I'm sure she and my dad are smiling down on us right now."

"Woof!" Millie wriggled between them and wagged her tail.

_____ Epilogue _____

Gardening teaches many lessons. The good news is, we remember a few.

SHHHH! IT'S TIME FOR THE SHOW! _Frank, turn it up so we can all hear._

"This is Jessica Robinson with your _Inside Houston_ report. Today _Inside Houston_ visits with Lucy Lake, author of the best-selling _Wisdom From the Garden._"

Did you hear that? Best-selling author? Lucy, can you believe it?

No, I hardly can!

"Tell us, Lucy, what was the inspiration for your book?"

"Well Jessica, all the credit goes to my mother, Barb Lake. When she died, she left behind her garden planner. When I realized how valuable the guidance I found there was for me, I decided to share her advice with others. Thus, _Wisdom From the Garden_ was born."

Your mother would be so proud!

Thanks Marisel. I hope so.

Woof!

Somebody put that dog out!

No, Daddy, she wants to watch.

"I understand this beautiful rose garden we're standing in now was created by your mother."

"That's right. This was her pride and joy."

"And who is this who's just joined us?"

"This is Millie, my dog and truly one of my best friends. Believe it or not, she's quite a gardener herself."

"I'm sure there's a story there. But right now, what can you tell us about these gorgeous roses?"

"We're standing next to the tea roses. Over by the fence are the chinas, next to the climbers. There's some rather rare antique roses by the shed."

"They're all beautiful. And the aroma! I only wish we could share it with our viewers."

"Thank you, Jessica. This is truly a special place. It's hard to believe that after my mother's death all of this was almost lost. Fortunately my fiancé is an expert on roses and he saved my mother's legacy."

"That would be Greg Polhemus of Polhemus Gardens? He's been in the news lately with his headline making partnership with Allen Industries."

"Yes, Greg's designed a water-wise, completely organic landscape plan for them that will really revolutionize their corporate campus."

"This comes on the heels of the adverse publicity Allen Industries received last year when Chemical-Free, Organic Metro Alliance called for a boycott of the company."

"Yes, when the company decided to seriously consider some of COMA's demands, they called on Greg because of his experience with eco-friendly landscaping."

"With your fiancé so busy and you touring extensively following the success of *Wisdom From the Garden*, when will you find time for a wedding?"

"We haven't set a date yet. We've talked about surprising everyone and running away to Vegas for the weekend."

Did you hear that, Frank? We can go to Vegas for their wedding.

You'd like Vegas. Lots of pretty showgirls.

You just let me catch you looking at showgirls, you old goat.

"And you do have a Vegas connection now, don't you?"

"That's right. My best friend, Gloria Alvarez is living out there now with her boyfriend, comedian Dennis Eddy."

"Speaking of someone whose career has really taken off lately..."

"Dennis has always been very talented. But with Gloria's help, he's developed a new style."

"What critics are calling activist comedy—highlighting serious social issues with humor. But let's get back to you—what are your plans for the future?"

"I'm contracted for a follow-up book, *Wisdom From the Kitchen*, incorporating some of my mother's recipes, as well as some specialties of my stepmother, Marisel Luna. Then I'll be working with Greg on a handbook of eco-gardening."

Name dropper!

She didn't get my name in there.

Sorry, Daddy. Next time. I promise.

"Sounds like you've really found a niche for yourself."

"I hope so. I'm certainly enjoying my new career."

"What do you think your mother would say about all this?"

"I think she'd say 'A garden brings out the best in everyone.' Even those of us who don't have green thumbs."

"On that note, viewers, we'll say goodbye. This is Jessica Robinson for *Inside Houston*.

Oh, that was wonderful! You looked so good on TV.

Lucy always looks good.

Spoken like a man in love.

Mmmm.

Now you've done it, Frank. They're getting all mushy again.

Hush, woman, and come give me a kiss.

I thought you'd never ask.

HARLEQUIN®

Temptation

THE WRONG BED

**What happens when a girl finds herself in the
wrong bed...with the *right* guy?**

Find out in:

#866 NAUGHTY BY NATURE by Jule McBride
February 2002

#870 SOMETHING WILD by Toni Blake
March 2002

#874 CARRIED AWAY by Donna Kauffman
April 2002

#878 HER PERFECT STRANGER by Jill Shalvis
May 2002

#882 BARELY MISTAKEN by Jennifer LaBrecque
June 2002

#886 TWO TO TANGLE by Leslie Kelly
July 2002

Midnight mix-ups have never been so much fun!

HARLEQUIN®

Makes any time special ®

HTNBN2

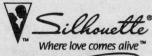

If you enjoyed what you just read,
then we've got an offer you can't resist!

Take 2 bestselling
love stories FREE!
Plus get a FREE surprise gift!

Clip this page and mail it to Harlequin Reader Service®

IN U.S.A.	IN CANADA
3010 Walden Ave.	P.O. Box 609
P.O. Box 1867	Fort Erie, Ontario
Buffalo, N.Y. 14240-1867	L2A 5X3

YES! Please send me 2 free Harlequin Flipside™ novels and my free surprise gift. After receiving them, if I don't wish to receive anymore, I can return the shipping statement marked cancel. If I don't cancel, I will receive 2 brand-new novels every month, before they're available in stores! In the U.S.A., bill me at the bargain price of $4.24 plus 50¢ shipping & handling per book and applicable sales tax, if any*. In Canada, bill me at the bargain price of $4.94 plus 50¢ shipping & handling per book and applicable taxes**. That's the complete price—what a great deal! I understand that accepting the 2 free books and gift places me under no obligation ever to buy any books. I can always return a shipment and cancel at any time. Even if I never buy another book from Harlequin, the 2 free books and gift are mine to keep forever.

151 HDN DU7R
351 HDN DU7S

Name	(PLEASE PRINT)	
Address	Apt.#	
City	State/Prov.	Zip/Postal Code

* Terms and prices subject to change without notice. Sales tax applicable in N.Y.
** Canadian residents will be charged applicable provincial taxes and GST.
All orders subject to approval. Offer limited to one per household and not valid to current Harlequin Flipside™ subscribers.
® and ™ are registered trademarks of Harlequin Enterprises Limited.   FLIPS03

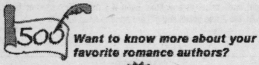

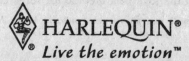

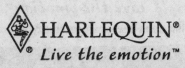